A flutter of something against the skin of her neck.

Fingers, caressing, stroking. Then a kiss, lingering, hot.

Nina's heart beat strongly in her breast and heat exploded pure and strong in her stomach.

She'd imagined this very scene countless times over the past few days. Had anticipated this moment. But nothing had prepared her for the thrill of the unknown that zinged through her bloodstream. The electric desire for the unknown, waiting, longing for touch, for connection to the stranger in her bedroom.

Dear Reader,

Best friends to lovers. One of our all-time favourite themes. But what would happen, we wondered, if a girl has two male best friends? Oh, the possibilities!

In *Shameless*, sexy baker Nina Leonard finds that she's turned into a serial monogamist, repeatedly mistaking one-night stands for the real thing. But when she receives an indecent proposal from hot best friends and business partners Kevin Weber and Patrick Gauge – namely to help her break her destructive dating pattern by arranging a night of anonymous sex with a fantasy stranger – Nina is hard-pressed to refuse. Especially since she's sure that stranger will be one of the two of them. But which one?

We hope you enjoy every erotic and neurotic moment of Nina, Kevin and Gauge's unconventional journey towards happily-ever-after. We'd love to hear what you think. Contact us at PO Box 12271, Toledo, OH 43612, USA, (we'll respond with a signed bookplate, newsletter and bookmark), or visit us on the web at www.toricarrington.net.

Here's wishing you love, romance and *hot* reading.

Lori & Tony Karayianni

SHAMELESS

BY
TORI CARRINGTON

MILLS & BOON
Pure reading pleasure™

*First published in Great Britain 2009
by Harlequin Mills & Boon Limited,
Eton House, 18-24 Paradise Road, Richmond, Surrey TW9 1SR*

© Lori and Tony Karayianni 2008

ISBN: 978 0 263 87480 8

14-0509

*Harlequin Mills & Boon policy is to use papers that are
natural, renewable and recyclable products and made from
wood grown in sustainable forests. The logging and
manufacturing processes conform to the legal environmental
regulations of the country of origin.*

*Printed and bound in Spain
by Litografia Rosés S.A., Barcelona*

TORI CARRINGTON

Multi-award-winning, bestselling husband-and-wife duo Lori and Tony Karayianni are the power behind the pen name Tori Carrington. Their more than thirty-five titles include numerous Blaze® mini-series, as well as the ongoing Sofie Metropolis comedic mystery series with another publisher. Visit www.toricarrington.net and www.sofiemetro.com for more information on the couple and their titles.

We dedicate this book to everyone
who's ever wondered "what if."
Here's to finding your own
unconventional happy-ever-after...

1

"IN THIS DAY and age, is it bad for a woman to yearn for some good, hot, anonymous sex?"

Nina Leonard sat back and took a sip from her extra-large white ceramic cup of latte, waiting for Kevin Weber and Patrick Gauge's responses. She'd intended her words to be shocking. Had wanted them to reflect the chaos she'd been feeling lately after a long period of unwelcome celibacy.

The three of them were seated around the mammoth fireplace that dominated the middle of BMC, the bookstore/music center/café they jointly owned in Fantasy, Michigan, southwest of Ann Arbor. It was just after ten and although the three partners had officially closed the front doors, three customers still roamed around the cozy depths of the store. One of them, an elderly woman with a cane, peeked at the three around a stand of marked-down holiday cookbooks and

Christmas CDs that would finally be packed away tomorrow when the calendar changed from January to February. The customer reminded Nina of her grandmother, bless her heart, who would have done exactly the same thing. But Gladys Leonard wouldn't have stopped at eavesdropping; she would have contributed something to the conversation. Perhaps she would even have sat down next to her to share her own erotic adventures, played out during the early Motown days of Detroit, a city that lay forty-five miles to the east of the small university town.

Nina was sprawled on the flowery, overstuffed sofa, her feet crossed on the coffee table in front of her, her large cup taking two hands to handle.

Lately, she'd been craving a man who would take two hands to handle.

"Uh-oh," Gauge said from the ottoman nearer the fire, where he sat tuning his acoustic guitar. "Have we hit the six-month mark already?"

Kevin put his own coffee mug down on the table next to the thriller he'd been reading. "Has it been that long already? Feels like just yesterday that we finally got rid of Mr. Jenkins."

Gauge chuckled. "That's because it *was* yesterday. That's when I spotted the sorry son-of-a-bitch browsing through the makeover section, you know, the one nearer the café."

"All the better to stalk Nina."

Nina gave an eye roll and rested her cup in her lap, her apron with the store's logo on the front still snowy white and feeling freshly starched. "You two think you know me so well." She tucked her short blond hair behind her ear. "I believe you know me not at all."

Gauge strummed a few chords of B.B. King's "The Thrill Is Gone" and looked at Kevin. "Correct me if I'm wrong, but didn't she say during lunch that we knew her better than anyone out there?"

"Mmm, yes. Just after we called her on her desire to go to Florida for Valentine's Day." Kevin glanced at her. "You love the snow and you know it."

"Are you calling me contrary?" Nina asked.

"Not at all."

"Wouldn't dream of it."

Nina took another long sip of her latte. This was usually one of her favorite times of the day, when the three of them drifted together, either at one of the café tables where they'd pick at what remained in the bakery display Nina had so carefully stocked, or in the music center where Gauge would pop in whatever blues or rock CD he'd received in that day's shipment, or here in Kevin's domain where original, leather-bound classics were stocked alongside the latest best-selling thrillers and romances.

But tonight…tonight Nina felt a restless something that wouldn't be calmed by the blazing fire in the stone hearth to her left, or by the thick, white snowflakes swirling golden under the old copper streetlamps she could see through the front window.

"I caught her browsing through the erotica titles in the romance section earlier," Kevin said.

Nina nearly choked on her latte.

"Ah, then that would explain it, wouldn't it?" Gauge asked, giving her a long, knowing look. "She's in need of a good orgasm."

"And in search of one, she'll wind up getting involved with the wrong man because she'll mistake the fundamental desire to mate for a relationship."

"What? Kevin Weber, you just did not use the word *mate*," Nina said.

"Better than *screw,* I think," Gauge said, putting his guitar aside and resting his well-developed forearms on his jeans-clad legs. He shrugged. "No matter the word choice, Kevin's right. How long has it been since we decided to combine our stores? Two years?"

"Three," Nina and Kevin said in unison.

"Yes, three. And in those three years, Kev here and I have watched you repeat the same cycle. First, there's all that wistful sighing and fidgeting—"

"I do not fidget." Nina caught herself scratching her shoulder and stopped.

Kevin sat forward. "Then there's the flirting with every half-decent-looking guy that comes through the front doors."

"I do not flirt with customers."

The two men shared a glance.

Gauge chuckled and shook his head. "Then she makes her choice, she goes out on one date, then two...."

Kevin took over. "She sleeps with him, thinks that now she's been intimate with the idiot, well, that constitutes a relationship...."

"And she spends the next six months trying to make something work that never stood a chance from the beginning."

"All because she wanted sex."

"And then it takes six months of her swearing off men before the cycle starts back up all over again."

Nina gaped at them both. "That is *so* not the way it happens."

"Yes it is," Gauge told her.

Kevin nodded.

Nina put her cup on the coffee table and then crossed her arms over her chest, staring at them.

Okay, so maybe they had a point. Maybe she was caught in some sort of vicious cycle that left her with exes stalking her from various areas of the bookstore, wondering what they'd done wrong. Only they hadn't done anything wrong. She had. She'd chosen men who held out zero hope of keeping her interest once the sex went bad.

And it always went bad, didn't it? She'd jump into the relationship, hormones raging, and they'd spend the first few weeks mostly in bed. And then slowly, but surely, things would begin to cool off from there. Then, inevitably, would come the day when the hormonally charged air would clear, she'd look at the man across the breakfast table and finally see him for what he really was.

And she would dump him.

Okay, she wasn't as cruel as all that. But she would find a way to wiggle out of it with excuses such as the café needed more of her attention, or she was thinking about going back to school, or she'd flat-out say that they'd probably made a mistake and maybe they should think about dating other people.

"Good thing the three of us are just friends," Gauge said. "Or else she'd have kicked both of us to the curb years ago."

"Mmm," Kevin agreed.

"That's only because I couldn't decide on which one of you to date, so I thought it would be a good idea not to date either of you."

Nina grinned, finally getting the shocked responses she was after.

KEVIN WEBER felt as though the neck of his white T-shirt had just shrunk three sizes, and he shifted the denim shirt he wore over it as he stared at the sexy blonde spilled over the couch like a satin sheet.

"What?" she asked with a wicked smile. "Surely you both knew I was attracted to you."

She looked between them and then her gaze settled on Gauge.

Kevin grimaced.

In the past three years he'd been in a constant state of lust where Nina Leonard was concerned. It was more than the clingy black pants and tight white tops she favored, showing her curvy body to perfection. Often he'd catch her stretching after a long, busy day when she thought no one was watching; there was something about the feline way she contorted her body, the back arches that alternately brought her lush bottom up and the smooth, tight-tipped swell of her breasts out, that had caused the loss of more than a single night's sleep.

Nina Leonard was smart, talented and witty. She could indulge in an hours-long open criticism of the classics while she tried out her latest sweets recipe and then dive into the latest celebrity gossip without missing a beat.

He knew everything about her. From her favorite color—deep purple—to the fact that her family was from an old, downtown section of Detroit and that she had settled in Ann Arbor after attaining her business degree from nearby University of Michigan. He knew that more than once she had burned a batch of her famous bear claws because she had her nose buried in one of those steamy romance novels, and that she preferred plain white underpants over thongs because wearing the latter found her constantly wiggling to try to remove what she called a permanent wedgie. (Now *that* had been a week to remember.)

And he knew that she considered him little more than an older brother she was constantly trying to fix up with one of her friends. She had once come straight out to ask if he was gay.

For the record, he wasn't.

And if he needed more reminders of that, all he had to do was think of the sudden tightness of his jeans when she admitted she'd been attracted to him.

Gauge slid him a knowing gaze. "We suspected."

Nina made a strangled sound. "You mean you guys talk about me in that…way?"

"Of course we do." Gauge crossed his own arms over his chest; he wore a T-shirt as Kevin did, but without a denim shirt to dress it up. Today he'd chosen a faded dark-gray one that advertised an old heavy-metal rock band. "We are just men, after all."

Kevin said nothing; in fact, he was incapable of saying anything at all.

He picked his coffee cup back up even as Nina took her feet from the table and sat forward, causing the front of her apron to bow open. Kevin gazed at the soft mounds of flesh visible in the deep V of her shirt and then back up at her face.

"So you both have thought about…sleeping with me?" she asked.

Kevin quickly put his cup back down, afraid he might choke if he tried to swallow anything.

Gauge openly considered her. "I don't know about Kevin, here, but you've landed the starring role in one or two of *my* favorite wet dreams."

Kevin stared at him and said, "Probably in concert with one or two other female participants."

Gauge shrugged without apology. "Here and there. I'm not going to hide that I'm a guy with varied tastes."

"As if you could," Nina said. "Nearly every woman who comes into this place always finds a way to linger in the music section."

"Hey, whatever sells CDs."

Kevin watched the two of them. Had Nina just given Gauge a suggestive smile?

And had she just turned that same smile on him?

He suddenly couldn't breathe.

"What about you, Kev?" she murmured. "Have you ever wondered what it would be like to have sex with me?"

POOR SAP, Patrick Gauge thought. *Look at him. He's about ready to jump out of his skin.*

Gauge shook his head and picked his guitar back up. Yeah, he'd freely admit that more than once he'd thought about dipping his fingers into the back waist of Nina's tight slacks when she gave him one of her generous hugs. He was only human. More, he was only a man.

Wasn't it his roving father who had explained to him that there wasn't one out there woman enough to keep a Gauge happy?

He absently strummed a few notes. He came from a long line of musicians who had traveled more than they'd stayed in one place. Recently, he'd been pondering how it was that three years had passed since he'd arrived in Ann Arbor and then Fantasy, with a plan to play a few gigs at college bars and then move on farther down the line.

But he didn't have to look too far for the answer. He took in his two best friends, the closest he'd come to any kind of real family, and he knew why he'd stayed. And why he continued to stay, trading a music career for selling CDs and working on a few CDs of his own that barely made it farther than the local college scene.

"I'd better go take care of the last customer," Kevin said in lieu of answering Nina's question.

Gauge shook his head again, having noticed that two of the browsers had left without buying anything, but the elderly woman who had kept her shopping close so she could listen in on their conversation had apparently been interested enough to add to her purchases.

He continued strumming an old blues tune that his father had taught him when he was seven until Kevin had followed the customer to the doors and locked them after her.

Kevin finally rejoined them, probably hoping that the conversation had moved on.

Gauge had purposely made sure it hadn't.

As soon as Kevin sat down, Gauge placed the bottom of the guitar on the area rug and gave it a twirl. "Hey, Nina, why don't you let Kev and I arrange that night of hot, anonymous sex you said you were looking for?"

2

NINA sat back into the couch as if pushed there by a man's commanding hands.

Gauge's grin was dirtier than anything a washing machine and a gallon of bleach could clean.

It seemed she wasn't the only one looking to shock tonight.

"Christ, Gauge, what is going on in that over-sexed mind of yours now?" Kevin asked, picking up the book he'd been reading and putting it in his lap.

"No, let him talk," Nina said, intrigued. "What *are* you suggesting, Gauge?"

The last thing on earth Nina wanted was to be predictable. Was it possible that her friends and partners were right and that she had been running in boring cycles for the past few years? Could her bad decisions begin as little more than basic, human need? Having gone without physical intimacy for months at a time, did desire cloud her judgment? Was she choosing men who were the most convenient based on their sexual attraction rather than on an equal balance of psychological and physical appeal?

While she wasn't one-hundred-percent ready to commit to the idea, she was willing to admit it might be a possibility.

Gauge gave her one of his easy shrugs, pulling his T-shirt a little tighter against his biceps. "Nina, honey, you need to get laid. It's as simple as that. And I think Kevin and I can help you there."

She looked back and forth between the two of them. "Do you mean…? Are you saying you think the three of us…?"

They stared at each other for long, heart-pounding moments.

"No…." Nina said.

"I don't think so," Kevin said.

"Actually that wasn't what I was proposing, but…" Gauge said.

Nina suddenly felt dizzy as she sank slowly back into the couch again.

Wow.

Okay, so her partners were hot. Gauge was John-Mayer attractive in a fundamental way that entranced women, who probably got home before they discovered they'd spent double or triple the money on CDs they'd never listen to while under his spell. He had a musician's easy style, his jeans looked as though they'd been made to fit him, his T-shirt held the right mixture of alpha-male dominance and devil-may-care appeal.

And she could look at his tattoos all day long and never tire of it.

Kevin, on the other hand, was Hugh-Jackman hot. Tall and slightly bookish, he had an easy grin and a set of washboard abs that she imagined he got through coaching hockey in the winter and soccer in the summer, because she never saw him doing anything more physical than what it took to unpack boxes and shelve books here. His big, dark eyes were the type a girl could lose her footing and fall into and never want to come out of again.

Yes, while she'd done her own share of bun-staring when they weren't looking, as she knew they both did with her, she'd never really considered what it might be like to sleep with either one of them.

As for both of them at the same time…

"No…." she said again, shaking her head.

Kevin looked at her curiously, as if surprised to think she'd even consider the idea of a threesome, and then looked at her again. "That's the most asinine thing I've ever heard, Gauge. While pop culture may have become more pornified in the past decade, that's *way* crossing the line for most people."

"You're right. You think the three of us argue during tax time now, just think what would happen if we slept together," Gauge said.

They continued staring at him. He put his guitar down and raised his hands. "It was a joke, all right?"

Nina didn't buy it.

"Okay, maybe it wasn't. And I'll be the first to admit that I've never considered guy-on-guy action." He appeared to shudder. "But I think I may be on to something here. Give me a minute."

Kevin rose and picked up his coffee cup and novel. "I'm not giving you another second. Look at the tension the mere suggestion of sex between any combination of the three of us is causing."

Nina waved for him to sit back down. "Hold on, Kev. Let's see where he's going with this."

"Got it," Gauge said, snapping the fingers of his left hand together. The knuckles bore the fading letters *L-O-V-E* he'd had tattooed on them when he was thirteen. "You don't sleep with us—"

Kevin interjected, "Smartest thing you've said all night."

"But we do arrange for you to sleep with someone…." He drifted off.

Kevin sat back down as if incapable of doing anything that required any sort of mental concentration at the moment.

Nina couldn't seem to drag her gaze from Gauge's striking face.

"Someone completely anonymous. No names allowed."

Nina twisted her lips. "But how do I know I'll be attracted to him?"

"What does it matter? You won't see him."

Kevin clasped his hands together between his knees as if trying to keep from slugging his friend. "What do you mean, she won't see him? If we arrange for her to go out with someone—"

"Ah, but that's where you're not getting me. I didn't say anything about her going out with someone, like on a date." He moved from the ottoman to sit in the chair next to Kevin's, putting him closer to them both. "This is about sex, can we all agree on that?"

Silence.

Nina didn't know how to respond.

"About fundamental human urges. Look, we all agree that Nina's made some bad choices because she has a tendency to go without for too long and then jump in too quickly as a result."

"Go without?" Kevin repeated.

Nina smiled. "No, no. He's got a point." She gestured with her hand. "Go on."

"So we set up something where you won't be able to see the guy, but he'll be able to see you."

"What, are you suggesting she be blindfolded?" Kevin asked, looking more and more dangerous. Nina found it interesting that Gauge appeared not to notice his friend's agitated state. Then again, maybe he did notice. He just didn't care.

"That's exactly what I'm suggesting." Gauge grinned and spread his hands wide as if his idea were the solution to all the world's problems. "Nina gets the hot, anonymous sex she's looking for…and we don't have to put up with some moron boyfriend hanging around for the next six months until she boots him out."

No one said anything.

"And then, maybe, with the whole sex element out of the way, she'll finally find some guy deserving of her," Gauge added.

Kevin got out of his chair and for a second Nina thought he might sucker punch Gauge. "That's the most ridiculous thing I've ever heard."

He instead turned to reshelf the book he'd been reading.

"Nina?"

She realized she'd been watching the fit of Kevin's jeans as he moved and blinked to look back at Gauge. He grinned at her.

"Would the guy be either of you?"

She'd intended the question to be as forthright as his suggestion. Instead it came out as a husky whisper.

She shivered all over, her nipples growing hard, her panties growing damp.

She'd never felt so wanton in her life. An idea like this was something more up her grandmother's alley—at least if you believed what she said when she talked about the old Motown days, and Nina did.

But now that the proposal was floating out there as a possibility, she found that she'd also never felt more turned on.

She looked at both of them leisurely. Took in Kevin's intense, soul-searching gaze. Pondered Gauge's sexy, suggestive grin.

"Well?" she asked, a fire igniting deep in her belly. "Would it?"

Gauge shrugged. "If it did include either one of us, you'd never know, would you?"

3

LATER THAT NIGHT, Nina lay back against her iron bedstead in her apartment above the store, staring at the ceiling. Her twenty-pound cat Ernest Hemingway's furry body curved against her thigh on top of the down comforter, his soft snores breaking the silence.

But it wasn't her cat she was mindful of just now. No, the suggestive conversation she'd shared with Kevin and Gauge was what dominated her thoughts to such a degree that she found it impossible to close her eyes.

Naughty images trailed through her mind one after another. First, there was Gauge holding himself above her, his hair framing his handsome face as he stared into her eyes. Then she blinked and his features were replaced by Kevin's full mouth as he leaned in to kiss her.

She caught her breath and groaned, tossing

the comforter off and covering Ernie with it. While the downstairs area of the old workspace had been completely updated when the three of them had joined forces three years ago, the two upstairs apartments had been left as is, the radiator heat hard to get exactly right. It was either too cold in her sprawling, two-bedroom place, or way too hot.

Of course, she recognized that her thoughts might be just as much to blame for her over-heated condition.

She licked her lips and threw her arm over her head, watching as Ernie freed himself from the blankets and twitched his tail at her before turning his back and jumping from the bed. She idly listened as his nails clicked against the areas of the polished wood floor not covered by rugs and then heard him crunching his dry food in the kitchen.

She couldn't remember the last time she'd spent a sleepless night thinking about a man. Correction, two men. Her best friends and business partners.

And if she had a brain in her head, she'd turn on the television in the corner and let Conan laugh her to sleep, putting a smile on her face that had nothing to do with either Gauge or Kevin or, Lord forbid, both of them at the same time.

What made secret fantasies special was that they were secret.

Okay, so, yes, she could admit to herself in the safety of her own bed, she'd had a dream once that had featured the two men in a way that had absolutely nothing to do with friendship or business. It had been last summer and on the heels of a memory that now stood out in stark clarity. The three of them had been at a garden party one of Kevin's late mother's friends had thrown. While everyone else gathered around the ice sculptures and buffet tables, they had changed into their suits and taken advantage of the Olympic-size pool nestled in a landscape designed to look like a mountain oasis. They'd been fooling around, splashing each other to break the boring monotony established by the stuffy gathering, then they'd graduated to dunking each other.

And then what had happened next had likely set the stage for what she was considering now....

"I don't know why women insist on buying bathing suits like the one you have on," Kevin had said of her red string bikini. "The way you keep having to rearrange the top or the bottom, it's obvious they weren't meant for swimming."

Nina had been adjusting the top; her right nipple was in danger of peeking out from behind the wet fabric. She'd watched as her skin puckered in awareness of Kevin's steady gaze, giving a little shiver as the material chafed against the sensitive tip.

Gauge's voice had sounded from behind her. "They don't buy them for swimming," he'd said, hooking a casual finger into the back of her suit bottom.

It was something he'd done at least a thousand times before. A teasing move not unlike what a brother might do. But in the wake of Kevin's comment on her suit and her reaction to his gaze, the air rushed from her lungs in a soft whoosh at the feel of his hot finger against her cool skin as he tugged her closer to him.

Kevin drew nearer her front. "So you're saying they buy them to drive men like us nuts, then?"

Nina was fascinated by the way droplets of water clung to Kevin's dark hair as he pushed it back from his face; she found it suddenly difficult to tread water. Abruptly she discovered that she wasn't only in the deep end literally, but metaphorically, as well. And when she felt Gauge press against her from behind, and Kevin from the front, she had the sensation that she was soon going to be in way over her head.

She grasped Kevin's shoulders to keep above the water at the same time as Gauge grasped her hips.

"Whoa there, sweetheart," he'd murmured against her ear. "We wouldn't want you to go under on us."

She'd restlessly licked her lips, her heart going a million miles a minute, her body flushed with heat despite the cool water as she considered what they might have in mind.

She felt Gauge's hands slide over her bottom and down the back of her legs even as Kevin reached for the arms she had around his neck for balance, her breasts pressed against the hard wall of his chest.

Then Gauge caught her foot and hoisted her up, catapulting her a few feet so that she hit the water face down.

The cad.

When she came back up for air, she sensed that she'd lost the battle with her top but didn't make a move to right it. Instead she merely stared at the two of them wickedly, watching them watch her as she allowed her body to float to the surface, her breasts partially exposed, the material of her suit bottom clinging to her swollen womanhood.

"You know, you're both right," she'd said as she slowly did the backstroke, coaxing both breasts out. "Women don't buy these kinds of suits for swimming. We buy them to drive the opposite sex wild." She'd leisurely licked her lips. "Absolutely, positively, stark raving mad."

And judging by both their heated expressions, she'd achieved her goal.

At least for one, sweet moment.

Then Kevin's mother's friend had come over to the pool to tell them the barbecue was ready....

Recovering from the memory to find herself not in the cool water of a swimming pool with two hot men, but in the middle of her empty bed while a winter storm raged outside, Nina groaned and rolled over, burying her face in her pillow. She hadn't thought about that time since it had happened. Okay, maybe she was lying. She had thought about it. Usually right around the time she was about to drop off to sleep and found her hand sliding down between her legs as if of its own accord to relieve a pressure there, brought on by the obvious absence of a man in her life.

The sheets were soft and warm and smelled of lavender. The mattress was newish and cradled her aching body. She pressed her hips against it and squeezed her thighs tightly together, relishing the tiny shivers that skittered over her. Her nipples throbbed, her breasts felt heavy and she couldn't seem to concentrate on anything other than the need screaming through her body.

Gauge and Kevin were right. She needed sex.

Merely thinking their names made her catch her breath, and she rocked her hips more solidly against the mattress. But the tight coiling deep in her womb refused to be satisfied by the vague action. So she slid her hand down and under her right hip, seeking the V of her thighs with her own fingers. She pressed against the swollen mound through her cotton underpants, but the impersonal touch only made her want more. So she worked her fingers under the top elastic, not stopping until the tips met with her shallow crevice. She was dripping wet. Stroking the damp folds, she found the engorged bit of flesh begging for her attention and pressed.

She climaxed instantly, caught off guard by her immediate and explosive response.

It usually took her a few minutes to reach orgasm.

Occasional masturbation almost always quieted her clamoring hormones.

But not tonight.

She extracted her hand from her underpants and rolled back over, more hot and bothered now than she'd been before.

Nina gulped a thick swallow and tightly closed her eyes, willing the unwanted emotions away. Wasn't life complicated enough wanting one man? What would she possibly do with two?

Her mind responded by offering up all sorts of interesting options.

Nina groaned just as Ernie leaped back onto the bed. She blinked at him standing at the edge of the mattress, staring at her, as if aware of what she was thinking.

"What?" she asked quietly. "Go to sleep and mind your own business."

If only she could do the same....

TWO DAYS LATER, Kevin watched Nina pass in front of the checkout counter, her snug black pants clinging to her delicious bottom, her white apron cinched at her narrow waist. She waggled her fingers at him and gave him the same wicked smile she'd been throwing his way for the past two days.

He rang up the amount on the register and distractedly quoted the total to the customer.

"Um, I think you made a mistake," Jeremiah Johnson said, staring at the display.

Nina moved out of view and Kevin ran the back of his hand across his forehead. "Pardon me?"

"You added a zero to the amount, I think." Johnson waved a book. "This should be $23.95, not $239.50. Unless the price on hardcovers went up again."

Kevin grimaced and mumbled an apology to the economics professor, canceling the transaction and starting again from scratch.

He didn't know how long he could take Nina's shameless flirting. While she'd always been friendly, often times bawdily so, she'd never downright tempted him the way she was doing now.

And his job performance was suffering for it. Over the past two days he'd gotten more orders wrong than right. Considering that he prided himself on customer service, his aberrant behavior only amplified his stress level.

He handed Johnson his purchase and apologized again even as Gauge walked behind the paneled counter and grabbed a few bags. "You know, one conversation will eliminate your sorry state."

"Shut the hell up, Gauge," he said under his breath.

But apparently not quietly enough because old Mrs. Christenberry stared at him in open-mouthed shock.

That was it. He and his friends were going to put this ridiculous topic to rest. Right now.

"Julie, man the register, please," he said to a part-time sales associate who was stocking books nearby.

He grabbed Gauge by the arm and led him in the direction of the stockroom. "You and I need to talk."

"It's about damn time."

He could say that again.

He opened the door, ushered his friend through it, and then stared at another associate who was stripping the covers off paperbacks to send back to distributors for credit.

"John, go see if the music center needs any attention for a few minutes, will you?"

The teen eyed him and a grinning Gauge and hastily left the room.

"Christ, Kevin, you're worse off than I thought."

Kevin stared at his friend. Gauge looked unaffected as he leaned against a table and crossed his feet at his booted ankles and then his arms over his chest. His T-shirt today was black and sported the logo from a Memphis House of Blues.

"This has got to stop. Right now," he said, pacing one way and then back again. "I can't eat, I can't sleep. I can't ban these…images from my mind."

"What images? Of Nina naked and moaning?" Gauge nodded. "Yeah, I'm going through pretty much the same thing."

Kevin stopped and fisted his hands at his sides. The idea that his friend felt the same way about Nina bothered him even more than the thought of his own agitated state.

"What? You believed you're the only one who's been suffering since our little conversation the other night?"

"But you've slept with two women since then."

Gauge grinned. "And your point is?"

"My point is that you're an asshole."

Gauge chuckled at that, nudging up Kevin's already soaring stress level.

Kevin grasped Gauge by the front of his

T-shirt, forcing him to uncross both his ankles and his arms.

"Whoa, watch it now." Gauge's smile disappeared briefly, the moment suddenly tense.

Kevin released him and took a long breath. "Sorry."

Gauge smoothed down his wrinkled T-shirt. "No need getting violent on me. I can set you up with someone if you're feeling that pent-up."

"No, thank you."

"You sure? Because I can guarantee you'll feel one thousand percent better tomorrow morning."

"No, *you* would feel better. I'd probably feel worse."

"But what if that person was Nina…?"

4

"THERE'S SOMETHING different about you," Nina's grandma Gladys said, pointing a red nail in her direction. "I don't know what it is, but rest assured, I'll figure it out before I leave here today."

Nina took a sheet of cookies out of the oven, placed them on the counter and then shook her hands out of the oven mitts she wore. "I don't have a clue what you're talking about. Everything is exactly the same as it was when we had lunch last week."

Liar.

Everything had changed. Not physically. But emotionally, Nina felt as if a door had opened, offering views out onto a lush vista she hadn't known existed.

All she had to do was step through that doorway and welcome the change.

And those emotional changes would then also become physical.

Through the round window in the kitchen door, she watched as Kevin chatted with Heidi Joblowski, her assistant. She gave an involuntary shiver.

"Ten years younger," Gladys said, her gaze following Nina's. "That's all I'd need and that man would have been in my bed aeons ago."

Nina nearly choked. "Ten years would make you sixty."

Her grandmother grinned. "Your point being?"

Her point being that there still would have been more than twenty-five years between her and Kevin.

Then again, her grandmother was probably right. She would have found a way, by hook or crook, to back Kevin—or any man she wanted—into her bed.

She shook her head.

Thankfully Gladys wasn't sixty anymore. She was seventy. And finally beginning to show it.

Nina hid a small smile as she took off her apron and then picked up the two plates she'd prepared. "Grab those soft drinks, will you? Our table's just been vacated."

Their table was the one for two in the far corner

of the café Gladys swore was the only place to sit. "All the better to see the hot young men you work with," she'd told her granddaughter.

Nina positioned the plates on the table and moved her chair so that she sat more next to her grandmother than across from her. She'd learned long ago not to block her view. Besides, there was always the risk of getting whiplash from Gladys asking her to quickly lean this way or that so she could get a better look at something, or rather, someone.

Of course, her grandmother had no way of knowing that she now shared her interest in her coworkers. Rather than cluck her tongue or put up her hand to ward off any unwanted comments on either Kevin or Gauge's posteriors, she intended to appreciate the view with her.

"So, are you done with your redecorating yet?" Nina asked, waiting until Gladys was seated and had placed her paper napkin in her lap, despite her casual surroundings.

She was long accustomed to her grandmother's oddball behavior. She might sit with perfect posture, but her sometimes purple hair, her hot-pink lipstick and her gold lamé jackets gave her an air of regal yet trashy pride.

Gladys waved her hand as she took a bite of her tuna salad sandwich on whole wheat. "That's been done for weeks. Where have you been?"

Right here. And she'd enjoyed three lunches with her since then. But Nina figured it was as good a place to start conversation as any. Urging her grandmother into a monologue about the fit nature of the handyman the decorator had sent to do the more difficult work—or the good-looking decorator himself, even if he did prefer men to women—would have gotten the ball rolling.

But her grandmother wasn't biting anything more than her sandwich as she watched Gauge entering the café for a cup of post-lunch coffee.

Her grandmother elbowed Nina so hard she almost fell from her chair.

"There he is."

Nina relaxed back in her seat, slowly chewing her own bite of tuna sandwich. Ah, yes, there he was, indeed.

A little thrill ran up her back at the memory of their conversation the other night combined with the interesting dreams she'd been having. She told herself she should be appalled, but her own recently awakened decadent side refused the response.

"He's a lazy lover, you can tell."

Nina nearly choked on her food. She quickly reached for her drink.

Gladys smiled widely. "Lazy, but his endurance would be out of this world. All day. And all night. That's my guess."

Nina watched the lines of Gauge's bottom in his faded jeans, and then appreciated the muscles of his back and arms in his snug black T-shirt.

She looked over to find her grandmother staring at her.

"If I didn't know better, girl, I would think you were giving him the lover's look."

"Don't be ridiculous," Nina said, hoping that her cheeks weren't as red as they felt. "Gauge and Kevin and I have been friends forever."

"And partners…"

"Business partners," Nina stressed. She shifted in her chair. "I talked to Mom yesterday."

Nothing was capable of derailing her grandmother more than mention of her daughter, Nina's mother.

In all the world, she didn't think there were two people less alike. Where her grandmother was a free spirit, her mother was as uptight

as they came, attending church three times a
week, working with Meals on Wheels and playing the role of perfect housewife to her father's
perfect corporate gentleman. While they weren't
wealthy, they were well-off. And her mother had
never worked a day of her life.

Her grandmother, on the other hand, refused
to let any man take care of her....

Of course, it probably didn't help that Gladys
called Helen her mistake.

Nina's mother had never liked the attention
that Gladys had showered on her granddaughter
from a young age. Growing up, Nina'd never
understood the feud between the two most important women in her life, but as she got older,
she'd come to realize that perhaps Gladys regret-
ted not taking more time out with her own
daughter, and was determined to rectify the
mistake by playing a significant role in her
granddaughter's life.

Then again, maybe the two women were too
different to ever have been close.

If that was the case, what did it say about her
and her grandmother? Could it be that Gladys
saw herself in Nina? And that's why she'd
formed the bond?

Or could she be trying to counteract Helen's influence so she wouldn't turn into a "dried-up old prune," as Gladys called Nina's mother?

Another elbow, another scramble to keep herself from falling off her stool.

"There's the other one."

Nina didn't have to ask to whom her grandmother was referring. She'd watched as Kevin joined Gauge at the cashier's counter in the audio section, apparently having finished his own lunch. Speaking of which, Nina looked down, surprised to find she'd nearly demolished the contents of her plate, as had her grandmother.

"Now him…he'd be a generous lover," Gladys said. "He'd be eager to please you. Loving."

Nina watched as Kevin leaned both hands against the countertop, his shirtsleeves rolled up, revealing the coiled muscles of his forearms.

"Do you think so?" she was surprised to hear herself ask.

Gladys's grin made her wish she hadn't said anything. "I don't think so, Nin. I know so."

Her grandmother made a play at wiping her mouth with her napkin, pushed her plate away, and then went about refreshing her lipstick. "So…which one are you looking to bed?"

"Grandmother!" Nina whispered harshly when a couple of women at a neighboring table gave them a hard look.

"Don't 'grandmother' me. I see those looks you're giving both of them. I wasn't born yesterday, you know." She put her lipstick and mirror away and closed her purse with a click. "And I know you."

Nina grimaced. She'd never credited Gladys with knowing her well. Gladys bought her only granddaughter bizarre Christmas and birthday gifts in garish colors that were more her own style than Nina's. Instead of taking her to Disneyland when she was kid, she'd taken her to the Windsor casinos, convincing the pit bosses that she was eighteen when she was only fourteen and earning her a spot at a blackjack table, which made things easier for Gladys because it meant she wouldn't have to go up to the room so often to check on her, although Nina hadn't played.

At least not until she did turn eighteen and could enjoy a hand or two on her own.

"They're my partners, Grandma, my best friends. I couldn't possibly get involved with either one of them," she said, but even she knew that there was no strength behind her words. Only a vague fear.

"You're also adults, Nina."

If only her grandmother knew what Gauge had suggested and what Nina was hoping the men would act on. The topic hadn't been mentioned again since that night. But, oh, how she wished it would be.

"Where are you going?" Nina asked, grasping Gladys's arm as she started to get up.

She was half afraid that her grandmother would make a stab at a matchmaking effort—if *matchmaking* was the right word for a connection that would only involve sex.

"I have a date for the matinee in twenty minutes."

Nina instantly relaxed. "It's not like you to make plans on our lunch day."

"I didn't." She smiled wickedly. "But since it looks like things are well in order here—" she spared the two men another glance "—very well in order, I'm going to give you the space you need to make your decision and go check out the new usher at the cinema. I hear his wife died last year. So that makes him prime mattress-boogie material."

Nina gave an exaggerated eye roll. "Do you ever think of anything other than sex?"

Her grandmother shrugged into her coat and smoothed down the front, appearing to give the question some consideration. "No, I don't. And seeing as at my age there aren't too many opportunities, I have to take full advantage of those that do come my way." She waggled a finger at her. "And it's nice to see that you're finally beginning to follow in your grandmother's footsteps."

5

"I'M NOT going to discuss this with you," Kevin said emphatically.

Gauge considered his friend who leaned against the cashier's counter. He'd been aware of Nina and her grandmother's attention on them ever since the women had sat down to eat their lunch.

"Then what are you doing here?" he asked.

What *was* he doing here? Simple. He wanted all this highly suggestive talk to end. Now. It had gotten to the point where he couldn't sleep, could barely eat, and fifty-nine minutes of every hour were spent fantasizing about what it might be like to claim Nina for one sweet night.

"I'm here to appeal to your better judgment to stop this. Right now."

Gauge pushed off the table. "Come on, Kev,

you know you've wanted Nina since the first moment you laid eyes on her. Here's your chance to have her. In a completely anonymous way."

"That's the part I don't like. If I…have her, as you put it, I want her with eyes wide open. Not shut."

"Well, then, I guess that means you'll never have her."

"What in the hell does that mean?"

"What do you think it means? You're the one walking around here with a constant hard-on, yet for the past three years you haven't had the guts to ask Nina out to a movie, much less to bed. That doesn't bode well for any future possibilities, Kevin, old boy."

Kevin felt like punching his friend. "Yes, I admit I may be attracted to Nina. But sleeping with her isn't even a remote possibility. There's more at stake here than my libido."

"Which makes the anonymous part all the more appealing. Because it puts the V in *viability*." He pointed at Kevin. "Think about it. You finally get to experience what both of us have been dying to taste…all without worry of the future of the business or our friendship because she won't know who she spent the time with. For all she knows, it could be a complete stranger. Some guy I came across at the bar."

"Don't you dare...."

"I didn't say I would."

"And what about you?" Kevin asked him. "Why don't you offer yourself as candidate?"

Gauge seemed to consider this. "I would, but..."

"But what?" Kevin waited impatiently.

Gauge grinned. "But I know you'd never forgive me."

"You're damn right about that." Kevin paced back and forth and then back again. "I can't believe we're even discussing this."

"So let's stop discussing it and make a plan."

"Not in a million years."

"What are you so afraid of, Kevin? That you won't be attracted to another woman if you sleep with Nina? May I remind you that your sex life is about exciting as a rerun of *The Brady Bunch*. You haven't been out on a date for more than a year—"

"Stay out of my sex life."

"I'd be happy to. If there were a sex life to stay out of." Gauge cursed. "Come on, man, what do you have to lose? The way I see it, you'd be doing

Nina a favor. And us. Lord knows the last thing anyone wants is for her to hook up with another loser we'll have hanging around the place for months until she comes to her senses again."

Kevin shook his head. "I can't."

"Fine, then. If that's the way you want it, I'll find someone else to take care of business."

"Yourself?"

Gauge shrugged. "Maybe. Maybe not. What do you care? Nina doesn't."

NINA WIPED the last corner of the counters and then leaned against it. The kitchen was a study in old-world charm and modern convenience, with thick wooden counters and hulking stainless-steel appliances. She shifted her watch from the inside of her wrist. Past ten.

She draped the wet cloth to dry, picked up her cup of decaffeinated latte and then stepped from the room, pushing open the door as she went.

The store was unusually quiet. Right about now she would normally hear the guys chuckling or talking wherever they'd decided to gather to unwind after a long day. But she heard nothing as she walked from the café into the music center and then into the empty bookstore. The front doors were locked and the Closed sign had been turned out.

Neither Kevin nor Gauge could be found anywhere.

Huh.

She took a long pull from the latte, wondering where they'd gotten to.

Actually, this was the third time in as many nights that this had happened. Ever since the night their conversation had turned toward all things suggestive. She felt slighted, missing the company of her friends.

It wasn't like them to leave without saying goodnight at least. It had become a ritual for them, a way to let the others know that no one was tending to the till in their area as well as a common courtesy. But neither of them had said anything to her.

Strange....

She stepped over to the gas fireplace, still blazing. She stared into the blue-green flames and sipped slowly from her cup. Probably she should just go upstairs, feed Ernie, and climb into bed with a good book after a long, hot shower. Only she didn't feel like leaving the shop just yet. Instead she turned toward the overstuffed couch, her favorite seat in the place, and sank down into the generous cushions.

Immediately she caught sight of a scarlet envelope in the middle of the table.

Nina's heart thrummed thickly. She leaned forward, tightly gripping her mug as she looked at the envelope. Her name had been printed neatly on the outside, leaving no doubt who it was for.

She looked around, trying to see if anyone was about, looking for her response.

There was no one.

Hands trembling slightly, she put her cup down and reached for the envelope, fumbling with it slightly before finally holding it in both palms and staring down at it.

It was still a good ten days before Valentine's Day, so she knew it had nothing to do with the holiday set aside especially for lovers. She ran her fingertip over the carefully written letters. She had little doubt that Kevin had penned it. She smiled, imagining the two men arguing over the envelope. She could see Gauge saying that they didn't have to write her name, that she would know who it was for, and Kevin debating that in a situation of this gravity, they shouldn't risk someone else mistakenly assuming the envelope was for them.

Both would have been right.

Nina settled back into the cushions and propped her feet on the edge of the coffee table, creating an easel with her legs against which she propped the envelope. She sat staring at it for long, uninterrupted minutes. She didn't have to wonder what was inside. She knew without looking.

They were taking the next step....

She realized she was holding her breath and let it out slowly, the action bringing little relief to her singing nerves.

Over the past few days she'd often found herself wondering about the change in climate around the store. She'd begun to question whether it had been wise even to discuss a union between the three of them. Because surely that one conversation was to blame—or to credit—for the change in their friendship.

But just like a hiker who'd found herself halfway up the mountain, it was easier to go forward than back. There was no retreat from such a journey once it was begun.

Were Kevin and Gauge as restless as she'd become? She'd wanted to ask them, but hadn't had the courage, afraid that perhaps they'd ignore the fact that the conversation had ever taken place. But there was difference in the way they both looked at her now. While there had existed a mild sexual interest in her movements, now she felt their gazes as surely as if they'd reached out and touched her.

But it wasn't until she surrendered her mind to her dreams at night that she got to play out a more intimate connection to one or the other, often both at the same time.

Until now.

Nina swallowed hard and turned the envelope over, noting that it had only been sealed at the end of the V. So simple to open.

Then why did she feel as if she were Pandora and that the contents of the envelope would forever change her life?

She absently worked her fingernail under the flap, the slight tearing of the seal filling the quiet store. She peeked inside to find a simple, white sheet of paper.

Simple. Now that was a word that didn't seem to fit the situation.

Then again, maybe it was custom-made for the state of affairs. Perhaps she was making far too much out of this entire thing. She might even venture a thought that she was doing exactly what the guys had originally accused her of, the entire reason for their discussion at all: the fact that she confused sex with love.

Is that what she was doing? Reading more into a simple matter that involved nothing more than the meeting of two needy bodies?

Nina dropped her head onto the sofa back. "Oh, for God's sake, Nina, just read the damn thing and get it over with."

For all she knew the letter would be a truce of sorts. A retraction of the offer and regrets that it had ever been extended to begin with. An attempt at a return to normalcy when everything had been far from it over the past few days.

She reached in and tugged the paper out, carefully opening it. It had been typed rather than printed. She smiled at the formality. Done to keep her from knowing which of them was speaking? She chanced a yes.

She licked her lips and smoothed the single sheet out and read:

Nina,
You are invited to a one-night-only, not-to-be-missed event. At midnight tomor-

row, leave your apartment door unlocked
and your inhibitions behind and put on the
enclosed blindfold…and nothing else….

Nina shivered all over. She picked up the
envelope again and looked inside. In the shallow
depths lay a single silk ribbon that didn't seem
wide enough to shield her eyes. She shook it
out, realizing that it was folded and that it was,
indeed, wide enough.

The slinky material warmed beneath her touch
as she raised it to her eyes and then fastened it
around her head. The front had been cut as a
mask, making allowances for her nose so that she
wouldn't be able to peek out the bottom.

For all intents and purposes she was blind.

Anticipation spilled over her like warm honey
as she sat for long minutes. Her own breathing
sounded loud to her own ears. She was keenly
aware of the thrum of her heartbeat. Made out
the sound of a car passing outside.

She gasped and quickly took off the mask.

Could she really do this? Turn herself over to
whichever one of them planned to enter her apartment? Put on a blindfold and trust that whoever
arrived would bring her pleasure and no pain?

Her throat tightened as she picked up the letter again.

Lights off, heat on, be prepared for the most erotic night of your life....

6

THE MINUTES of the day ticked by with agonizing slowness. Nina stared at the clock, willing the hands to move, for the day to be over so that she could rush headlong into the mysteries of the night.

"Is the second batch of bear claws ready?" Heidi asked as she came into the kitchen.

Nina blinked, forgetting for a moment where she was. Half an hour had passed, and she still hadn't made the glaze for the fresh batch of treats.

"No," she said, turning instead to a plate of frosted heart-shaped cookies baked in honor of Valentine's Day. "But these are ready."

Heidi sighed. "I don't know what's going on with the three of you today. I swear, if it weren't for Brad, John, Julie and I, this place would probably close down."

Nina rushed around the table. "How do you mean?"

Heidi blinked. "Just look at you. You're acting like you're suffering from advanced stages of Alzheimer's. And I hear the same thing is going on with both Kevin and Gauge."

Nina's tongue seemed suddenly too big for her mouth. "Both of them?"

"Are you going to make me repeat everything I say?" She shook her head. "Forget it. You probably aren't listening to me, anyway."

She left the room and the door swung back and forth slightly before finally coming to a rest.

Of course, Heidi was right. She wasn't listening. Had stopped listening the instant the girl had said that both Kevin and Gauge were as distracted as she was.

Could it be...? Was it possible that...?

She squeezed her eyes tightly closed and forced herself to walk to the other side of the table. Wasn't it bad enough that she'd barely slept since last night? And that when she had finally drifted off, her dreams had been so vivid that she'd have sworn they were real?

God, just look at her. She was a wreck. She'd forgotten to set her alarm and had been late this morning, forgoing her usual shower as she hurried to get dressed to unlock the store, today being her day to open. She'd pulled her hair back into a ponytail and wore only minimal makeup, determined to throw herself into work to help the time fly by.

Instead it seemed at a standstill.

She sighed heavily and tried to focus on making the glaze for the bear claws.

IF THE DAY had passed by with agonizing slowness, then the moments leading directly up to midnight were pure torture. Nina knelt in the middle of her bed, the blindfold tied tightly, the material of her nightgown rasping against her breasts with every deep breath she drew in.

She'd been told to wear nothing, but she'd been incapable of obeying that rule if only because she felt vulnerable enough already with her eyesight taken from her.

And she was acutely aware of every part of her body. From the soreness of her palms where she'd chosen to hand-knead bread dough in an effort to alleviate some of the anxiety pushing from the inside out, to the backs of her thighs and her buttocks from her lunch-hour workout at Silver's Gym, giving the new treadmill a run for its money, to her sore toes, from new athletic shoes that hadn't yet been broken in.

She heard Ernie scratching against the closed kitchen door. He gave a soft meow. Nina imagined him twitching his tail and turning to curl up on the large pet pillow she'd placed in the corner for him.

She couldn't see and didn't want to chance that either she'd step on him, or that he might attack whoever appeared at her door.

While the day had been long and busier than usual, she'd spent the better part of the past three hours doing nothing other than preparing for this moment. Getting ready for the night to come. Not just physically, but mentally. This was so outside her normal mode of operation as to be ridiculously close to the dreams she'd been having.

But as she soaked in a fragrant bath and methodically shaved her legs and the sensitive skin between her thighs, she slowly gave herself over to the idea that she had to do this. Had to give herself over to her more primal side if only this once, to be wanton and decadent. Had to see if she possessed the daring that her grandmother had in spades.

Music. She should have put on music.

Nina slightly loosened the blindfold and had begun to get up when she heard footsteps in the hall.

Her heart racing, she quickly retied the blindfold and climbed back into the middle of the bed, repeatedly smoothing her hands over her silk-covered stomach.

She knew a moment of fear as she listened to the outer door open and then close again. What if the man was neither Kevin nor Gauge? She hadn't given the idea any great amount of consideration. Not since the night they talked. She'd automatically assumed that it would be one of them.

But what if they'd sent someone else?

She reached for the blindfold again.

"No, don't," a low male voice whispered.

She shivered, not realizing he'd entered the bedroom until she heard him speak. She tilted her head slightly, not recognizing the voice. Of course that meant little, because she'd never heard Kevin or Gauge speak in a husky whisper.

She felt a brush of hands on her arms. She gasped at the innocent touch, her every nerve ending catching fire.

The hands urged her to stand.

Nina did as he bade, slowly scooting to the

edge of the bed. Her bare feet met the cool wood floor. She stood, seeking the warmth of the nearby rug, suddenly all too aware of her blindness.

Her shallow breathing sounded loud in the quiet room.

"Are you still here?" she whispered.

"Mmm." A hum was her response, coming from behind her when she'd expected it in front of her.

What was he doing? Was he looking at her? It seemed the only logical explanation given that she heard no sound. He had to be taking in the lines of her nightgown, perhaps put off that she'd chosen to wear something rather than wait completely naked as requested.

She felt heat against her neck and she automatically tilted her head to allow him greater access, her breath exiting in a soft hiss. She was hyperaware of everything, she guessed because she could see nothing. He smelled not of cologne but rather of the winter night and snow and the fresh Michigan air. She tried to match the scent to the man, but her mind refused to cooperate, overwhelmed instead by the signals her body sent it.

She was preoccupied with the fact that he stood so close behind her.

A flutter of something against the skin of her neck. Fingers, caressing, stroking. Then a kiss, lingering, hot.

Nina's heart beat strongly in her breast and heat exploded pure and strong in her stomach.

She'd imagined this very scene countless times over the past few days. Had anticipated this moment. But nothing had prepared her for the thrill of the unknown that zinged through her bloodstream. The electric desire for the unknown, waiting, longing for touch, for connection to the stranger in her bedroom.

Every man she'd ever had a relationship with had been an open book. Easily readable, easily understood…predictable.

This…this mystery made her both long to jump out of her skin and run from the room.

The hands slid from her shoulders down over her arms, eliciting tiny shivers as they went. Nina could do little more than stand ramrod straight. It was all she could do to concentrate on her breathing. In…out. In…out.

This was insane! She couldn't possibly do this. It was too strange, too unfamiliar. She wasn't at all made up like her grandmother Gladys and she'd been stupid to even think she was.

She began to turn around, her intention to lift the blindfold and call things off.

The hands found her hips and grasped her solidly, pulling her back against a tall, hard body.

Dear Lord in heaven, she suddenly couldn't name the current president if she tried.

The heat of his body warmed her silk nightgown, the undeniable hardness of his erection pressing against the top of her buttocks. She threw her head back against the shelf of his shoulder, covering his hands with hers. He moved, drawing the silk up, the hem climbing her legs, sweeping up over her thighs, the cool night air hitting her exposed skin as he went. The hem finally reached her upper thighs and fingers, probing, intimate, slid between her legs and the slick, bare flesh waiting there.

Nina's knees threatened to give out at the brazen move even as she fought to catch her lost breath. She wasn't sure what she'd been expecting. More foreplay. More seduction.

Instead, he'd gone straight for the prize, long, thick fingers stroking the length of her womanhood.

She caught her nightgown in her own hands, holding it aloft, giving him easier access so that he could carry out his intentions. Her rapid breathing brought her breasts against the silk, making her aware of the hypersensitive state of her hard nipples.

The fingers disappeared from her tender flesh and she moaned in protest as he caught the hem of her gown and stripped it off over her head.

All at once, Nina became aware of her complete nakedness…vulnerability. It was all she could do to stop herself from clutching her arms around her sensitive areas.

The notion was banished to the far corners of her mind as he pulled her back flush against him again…and she realized that he, too, was completely nude.

Her knees did give way. He caught her, pressing her even more solidly against his hot erection.

She'd never felt so alive. So bonelessly needy.

One of his hands moved back to stroke her between the legs, the other circled her waist, budging upward so that he both supported her rib cage and caressed her breast with calm assurance.

The fingers between her legs were doing all sorts of wonderfully amazing things. They moved over the shallow crevice, lightly probing, and then dipped between the swollen folds of flesh, her slickness lubricating his deepening strokes. He caught the bit of flesh at the top and she shuddered, shocked to find herself near climax.

He seemed to sense her turned-on state and abandoned the bud to her quiet protests, moving his fingers instead toward her tight, wet opening.

Nina held her breath, waiting, longing....

He bypassed the portal and moved farther along.

She regained control of her motor skills, her knees growing stronger under her even as he pinched her nipple and then spread his palm around the mound of her breast, squeezing, his other hand continuing to tease her womanhood.

She caught the hand in both of hers, forcing it away and hauling it up to her mouth. The hard male member pressing against the top of her buttocks seemed to jerk as a result. She brought his fingers to her mouth, putting them against her tongue one by one, and then sucking on them, dampening them. She tasted her own musk there on his skin.

Then she moved the hand back between her legs, leading his index finger to her portal, hesitating only slightly before encouraging it to breach her tight flesh.

She moaned even as his groan filled her right ear. He nipped at her neck as she bore down against his finger, her hand no longer guiding. He thrust the thick, long digit up into her waiting body and then slid it slowly back out. She groaned her protest at its sudden absence and then gasped when he reentered with two fingers, his thumb drawing tight circles against her clit.

Nina's body shattered into a thousand shimmering pieces as she succumbed to the liquid sensations rushing through her, completely supported by his strong arms.

Sweet hell....

Unable to use her sight to search his face, to see what his needs might be, how he interpreted her orgasm, she allowed herself to ride the wave of sheer emotion to the end, relishing every last lick of heat and sensation to its sugary finale.

Had she ever had such a powerful climax? Felt so uninhibited? No. Of course, she realized that the absence of an important sense likely amplified her other senses, but she didn't think credit was completely due to the blindfold. Rather, she suspected the license she'd given herself to be as bad as she wanted to be had a lot to do with the heightening of her feelings.

The blindfold had merely served as an aid toward that end.

The scent of rubber reached her nose. She breathed it, becoming aware that he'd released his hold on her and that she was standing on her own.

She shivered in anticipation as she listened to him roll the condom down over his length.

And then she discovered firsthand just how long his member really was....

7

NINA HAD NEVER felt more outside herself…so part of the world that surrounded her, an extension of everything rather than an independent part. She trembled violently as strong hands claimed her bare hips, bringing her bottom against an erection that surely couldn't be as large as she suspected. Curiosity getting the better of her, she slid her hand between them, curving her fingers around the rubber-covered steel.

She swallowed deeply. He was larger than any man she had encountered before, inspiring fear of whether she could handle his size.

He groaned, his fingers digging into the flesh of her hips possessively. Nina freed her hand and he positioned his member between her thighs, sandwiching himself there, stroking her with his erection where minutes before he had used his fingers.

She threw her head back and moaned, the heat surging upward. Fear fled, leaving in its wake pure, unadulterated need. The hands left her hips, heading down her lower belly until she felt him from behind and in front. He stroked her even as he parted her flesh, opening a place for him in her shallow channel. Using his hand, he moved the head of his erection to rest against her portal.

She caught her breath, preparing herself even as he paused.

Everything stopped for a heartbeat. He didn't move. She didn't move.

Then he was breaching her.

Liquid fire ignited along Nina's skin, flashing down and then up again. He dipped in a few millimeters, then withdrew, and repeated the process again, as if methodically stretching her muscles to accommodate his length and girth. Her knees buckled slightly and he caught her, bending her forward a few inches so that he had better access.

And the instant she expected him to withdraw, he surged into her to the hilt.

She climaxed immediately, squeezing him deep inside her.

Nina couldn't remember a time when she'd

been so orgasmic. To wish for one mind-blowing crisis had sometimes been too much. And here they had barely started and she'd come twice already.

He'd held still as she exploded around him, but now he moved again. Nina shuddered with every stroke. She wasn't so much concerned if she could handle his size anymore; now she was worried she wouldn't survive her own excitement.

She moved her right hand to rest against her knee and used her left to reach behind her, flattening her palm against his washboard abs. She felt trembling there at her touch. She nudged her fingers downward, finding the root of his shaft and squeezing even as he thrust into her again.

So good....

Sweet sensation flooded her, swirling upward into a red cloud of desire as each thrust urged her to yet another destination she longed to see, to experience. It soon took too much concentration to hold him, so she released her grip and used both hands to balance herself, tilting her bottom up even more. She was rewarded with a thrust so deep she thought he'd touched her heart.

The hands on her hips tightened and he stiffened, his groan telling of his impending climax.

Nina helped him along by moving herself down his length and then bearing down on him again, pushing him right over the edge.

For long moments afterward, they stayed like that, him curved along her back, holding her tightly.

When her mind finally began to clear, she experienced a moment of embarrassment. She was not an inexperienced woman at all. But so far she'd acted the hesitant virgin on her wedding night.

She gently grasped the hand that still stroked her intimately, along with his other one, and loosened his grip so that she could turn around in his embrace.

Using her fingers, she found his mouth, and then kissed him long and hard, rubbing her throbbing womanhood against him, the tips of her breasts tingling where they met the wall of his chest.

His fingers fluttered against the line of her jaw, gently caressing, lending a certain affection that stilled her heart to the moment.

Only she wasn't looking for affection.

"My turn," she whispered, pushing him down onto the bed.

She couldn't see him. But at this point she didn't need to. She relied on her remaining senses to guide her along her path, running her fingertips over the springy hair of his thighs until she found his semihard erection. She smiled and licked her lips, carefully removing the used condom and feeling around for the packets she'd put on her bedside table. She found one. But rather than putting it on, she nudged him farther up the bed and then climbed up on top of him, cradling his legs even as she caressed him with the top sheet and then bent to taste him.

Mmm....

Evidence of his need coated the thick knob. She ran her tongue against it, then fastened her mouth on it and sucked, lightly swirling the tip of her tongue around the lid even as her right hand fastened around the base. His erection immediately stood at full attention, rebounding from his climax. She heard his low growl and felt his hands on her shoulders, but she ignored him, moving her mouth farther down his heavy shaft. There was no way she could take all of him, but she could use her hands and mouth in combination to bring him pleasure.

"Move around," he whispered harshly, using

his hands to indicate what he meant by gripping her right leg and tugging.

Nina removed her mouth and allowed him to reposition her so that her thighs were on either side of his head and she was even with his erection. She happily went back to work, the air exiting her lungs in a rush when she felt his hot mouth on her most delicate area.

Dear Lord....

She nearly climaxed on the spot.

He made a low growling sound again and then grasped her bottom, drinking from her deeply and distracting her from her intentions. It was all she could do to continue as chaos built up anew in her womb, threatening to explode at any second.

She began to wonder if she'd survive him at all. What impact did so many orgasms in such a short time have on a woman? Was her health in peril?

She jerked upright, prepared to rush headlong into her next crisis. But he removed his mouth one moment too soon.

Nina made a sound of protest even as she found herself being turned over on the bed, instantly trapped by the weight of his body above her. She heard the sound of the foil package being opened and smelled the latex mingled with the scent of both of their sexes, and before she knew it he was surging up within her again.

Her back came up off the mattress as she took him in.

He stroked her again…and again…and again…making her call out in unabashed pleasure as a ball of heat grew larger and larger within her, turning and spinning out of control. He slid his hands under her bottom and held her still, thrusting deeply into her. And then he moved his hands to the backs of her legs, urging her legs up until her knees were folded against her chest.

Nina caught her breath. This normally wasn't a position she liked. She generally preferred to give as much as she got. And being folded like this dictated that she be still. She began to protest…until she felt his member stroke her G-spot in a way it had never been touched before.

Then his mouth was on hers. Gently coaxing.

For the third time, wild orgasm took hold….

WEAK WINTER SUNLIGHT cut a swath across Nina's bed and her face, whispering for her to waken. She slowly blinked open her eyes, feeling as if she was floating in a cloud of soft, warm cotton. She allowed her lids to drift shut again, growing aware of things one by one.

First, her body ached in a way that it had never ached before. Her delicate areas were beyond sensitive and swollen, her inner thighs bore what felt like stubble burn, and her breasts were overly tender. She smiled languidly, experiencing a sense of morning-after bliss unlike any she'd ever achieved.

She blinked open her eyes again, just then realizing she wasn't wearing the blindfold.

Somewhere in the middle of the night, after climaxing so many times she'd lost count, she'd drifted off to sleep in her mystery lover's arms, the blindfold still firmly in place.

Now she felt around the top of her head, and her neck, thinking it must have come loose while she slept. Out of the corner of her eye she caught sight of something black. She turned her head to see that the blindfold had been laid against the other pillow.

She reached out and fingered the silken material. Had he taken it off her? It stood to reason that he had, since she'd tied the knot tightly and now both ends were open. And the way it perfectly rested against the white pillowcase told her someone had laid it there.

Her heart skipped a beat at the thought of being watched while she slept, sans blindfold. Strange, really, since she hadn't minded being watched while they'd indulged in sex.

Maybe it was because she'd missed the opportunity to see who had been the master of those hands and that magnificent body.

Had he thought her aware and wanted to reveal himself?

She crumpled the mask in her hand and brought it to rest against her chest under the comforter, smiling secretly even as a hot flush claimed her cheeks at the memory of all that had passed the night before.

She'd gotten a copy of the *Kama Sutra* from her grandmother one year for Christmas. She'd been seventeen and still at home and her mother had nearly had a heart attack when the gift was unwrapped. It was all Nina could do not to choke at the grossly inappropriate holiday gift. But Gladys had argued that she wasn't a child anymore and that there was nothing dirty about sex. And the sooner she learned the right way to do it—even if it was only through the diagrams in the book—the better.

Her mother had confiscated the book and

Nina had rescued it from the bottom of the kitchen garbage can later that night, tucking it into the bottom of her stationery box where her mother would probably never see it. The biggest risk of discovery was when she'd told her parents goodnight and pored over the illustrated pages alone in her bedroom.

Thankfully her mother had never found out about the book. And Nina herself hadn't seen it for a number of years.

But last night she was pretty sure she'd accomplished a good percentage of the positions outlined.

She smiled again and snuggled deeper into the blankets.

Bless Kevin and Gauge's little hearts. They'd been right. Pure, anonymous sex had been exactly what she'd needed. And then some.

Now, the problem lay in figuring out which one of them she'd spent the night with....

She heard scratching coming from the direction of the kitchen. Ernie. Nina laughed and then rolled closer to the edge of the bed. Thankfully, she didn't have to be in the shop until later that morning, since it was a Saturday and she'd arranged for Heidi to handle everything until she got in.

But she felt so good she thought she might go in, anyway.

And see which of her two partners was in as bad…or as good a shape as she was.

AN HOUR LATER, she sat at the counter in the café section, staring into the depths of her coffee cup.

"More?" Heidi asked, holding up a coffeepot.

Nina shook her head and sighed, looking over her shoulder to see if either Kevin or Gauge had made it in yet.

She'd come down expecting to find them both at work, making her job of figuring out which one of them had visited her easier. But neither one of them was in. And neither was expected in until later that day.

Strange….

Few and far between were the times when all three of them hadn't been present at the shop— mostly because it had taken some time to pay back the loan they had taken to combine the three stores and put them solidly in the black. But now that they had a staff of three that they rotated, they had the luxury of missing a day or two here and there. Only they had never done it at the same time.

Nina pulled her cell phone out of her apron pocket and checked the display. No missed calls. Of course, she would have felt the vibration had someone called, but that wasn't the point.

She scrolled through her numbers. Gauge's name came up first.

Her thumb hovered over the call button. Then she sighed and closed the phone again, putting it back into her pocket.

Sneaky devils. They'd probably planned it this way so she couldn't play amateur sleuth and figure out which of them had given her so much pleasure.

8

MUCH LATER that day, after the last of the customers had finally left the building, Nina closed and locked the front doors and turned the Closed sign around. And then she smiled.

Reckoning time.

She turned around with purpose and strolled toward the café where she'd watched first Gauge, and then Kevin, go, helping themselves to the display cabinet.

She walked into the room to find them sitting side-by-side at the counter eating bear claws.

Nina rounded the counter and crossed her arms, staring at them both.

Gauge sat back and grinned.

Kevin blinked at her and grimaced.

"Have a nice night, Nina?" Gauge asked, openly considering her.

"Why don't you tell me?" she said, leaning

her palms on the cool tile. "I mean, wouldn't you know that as well as I?" She took in his suggestive expression and his relaxed posture and then moved her gaze to the man next to him. "Or are you the one who would know that, Kevin?"

He grumbled something under his breath and pretended an interest in his coffee.

"What was that?" Nina asked.

Gauge's chuckle drew her attention back to him. "You know better than to think it would be that easy, Nina. Deal was that you wouldn't know who paid you a visit last night. And that you'd never know."

Yes, that was part of the deal. But she was reneging on it. She needed to know who had rocked her world. Partly to give him thanks. Partly so that she could get more where that had come from.

"Both of you were scarce this morning."

"Yeah, we heard you were looking for us," Gauge said. "I had meetings in Ann Arbor with a distributor."

"Mmm," Nina said. "I just bet you did."

Gauge finished off his claw and wiped his mouth casually with a paper napkin. "You know, Nina, what you're leaving out of the equation is that your midnight lover might have been a stranger."

Kevin shifted on his stool. "Can we just drop this?"

"We're not dropping anything," she said. "As for the stranger part, Gauge, I know he wasn't a stranger. He knew me too well to be a stranger." She slid her gaze between them. "Which means that it had to be one out of the two of you."

Again, the scowl from Kevin, the grin from Gauge.

She sighed. Well, that hadn't worked, had it? She'd set out to find which one of them had made the earth move for her and she was being stonewalled.

Which was only fair, a small voice told her. She'd agreed to the terms wholeheartedly when they'd been extended to her. Just because she wanted to change the arrangement didn't mean they did.

"Are we going to talk about anything else?" Kevin asked. "Because there are a couple of business matters I'd like to discuss."

Nina and Gauge stared at him.

He sighed heavily. "Fine. I'm calling it a night then."

He pushed from the counter.

Gauge wiped his hands with his napkin and then hit a perfect shot into the garbage can, rising as well. "That means I'd better wrap things up, too."

Nina planted her hands on her hips. Hips that bore trace marks from the fingers that had held them last night. "Oh, no you don't," she said, coming from around the counter. "You two aren't going anywhere until we have this out."

"There's nothing to have out," Kevin said, getting his coat from the back room and handing Gauge his leather jacket.

They both shrugged into their respective garments as they headed toward the back door where their cars were parked.

"Get back here this minute," Nina demanded, following them.

She stopped and let out a long breath. "Come on, guys, you can't just leave me hanging this way. I've got to know which one of you it was."

Gauge was shaking his head. "Nothing doing, sweetheart." He bent in and kissed her cheek.

Nina closed her eyes, trying to discern whether it had been his kisses that had bruised her lips.

"Told you she'd try to misinterpret sex for a

relationship," Kevin said, leaning in to kiss her other cheek.

She blinked her eyes open, trying to figure out if it had been him.

"Goodnight, Irene, goodnight," Gauge said, holding the door open for Kevin.

He walked through it and Gauge followed.

Nina caught the door before it could close.

"Give a girl a break!" she called after them, Kevin going right, Gauge left.

"I thought we already did that," Gauge said, his chuckle echoing in the still, cold winter night's air.

Kevin opened his car door. "Goodnight, Nina. See you in the morning."

As both of them pulled away into the night, Kevin in his conservative Honda, Gauge in his vintage Chevy, Nina stood stock-still, watching after them.

Then she released a sound of frustration that only she could hear.

BY ALL RIGHTS, the midnight rendezvous should have calmed Nina's dream life. But three nights later, with little luck in unearthing who her visitor had been, she was still indulging in decadent dreams that left her waking up hot and bothered and more than primed and ready for Round Two.

She should have peeked, damn it. She should have lifted the blindfold at some point and found out who her lover was.

But she hadn't. And for the past four days she'd been an emotional wreck, thinking one moment that Gauge was the man, the next that it had been Kevin.

And now that she was sitting with her grandmother for their weekly lunch, she was this close to blurting the entire story out to Gladys, desperate for advice.

"He sent me flowers yesterday," her grandmother was saying as she dug in to her chicken salad. "Roses. Red."

"Who?" Nina blinked.

"Harold, of course." She stared at her. "Haven't you heard a word I've been saying?"

Nina waved her hand over her bowl of homemade minestrone. "Of course I have."

Her grandmother's wide smile made her wince. "Okay, out with it. Who is he?"

Nina grumbled into her soup. "I don't know. That's the problem."

"So you're in this agitated state because of a

man you've never met? Must be some man. What, was he a customer?"

Nina shook her head, wondering how much she dared tell her. "No."

Gladys threw her napkin to the table. "Out with it, girl. I'm too damn old for the game of cat and mouse."

Nina stared at her grandmother. It was like her to be so short. "It's nothing. Like you said. Just some guy who came into…the store. I don't even know who he is. But…" She bit hard on her bottom lip. "But I've been having some interesting dreams about him ever since."

Gladys laughed quietly. "Sometimes dreams can be better than the real thing."

"Not in this case, they aren't."

Gladys's smile widened. "Uh-huh. I thought you had that well-sexed look about you when I came in. So you've finally gone and done what I've been telling you to do for years and indulged in some anonymous sex." She reached over and squeezed Nina's hand. "Good for you. I'm proud."

Nina found it odd that Gladys couldn't have been talking about her being granted with an award for something.

She grimaced.

"What did he look like? I bet he was hot."

Nina nearly choked on the spoonful of soup she'd taken.

Gladys rubbed her left arm before she picked her napkin back up and resumed eating. "Damn age. I reached for a box of cereal off the top of the refrigerator this morning and must have pulled a muscle." She shook her head. "Although it could be worse. Violet— You remember Violet, don't you dear? My friend from bingo? Anyway, a month back she broke her hip just walking out her front door."

Nina was desperate to change the subject. "So who's Harold?"

Gladys's smile returned. "You remember that usher I told you about last week?"

"Ah, yes. The one that's been widowed a year and is prime…um…dating material."

"That would be him." Gladys crunched on lettuce and swallowed. "Anyway, I went to that movie. Only I didn't see any of it. Harold and I sat in the back row making out the whole time."

Nina gaped at her, trying to imagine her seventy-year-old grandmother making out in a theater with an equally old man.

Eeeew.

"Don't worry. It wasn't a regular cinema. It's one of those old places that shows old movies. *Casablanca* was playing and there were only about five people in the place. All my age. Well, except for the one young guy. But he didn't even notice us."

Nina held up her hand. "I could do without the imagery."

Gladys laughed. "Seems sex hasn't loosened you up any."

She had her there. Sex *hadn't* loosened her up. It had only served to make her more frustrated. Although for an entirely different reason.

Her grandmother rubbed her left arm again.

"Maybe you should have that looked at, Nana."

Gladys shook her head and sighed. "I have my regular appointment next week. Whatever it is can wait until then."

Just then Heidi came up to the table. "Sorry to interrupt, Nina. But there's a minor emergency in the kitchen…."

Nina told her assistant that she'd be there in a minute and waited as Gladys finished her salad, wiped her mouth and then reapplied her lipstick. "It's just as well. I've got another date with

Harold." She smiled as she clicked her purse closed. "*Doctor Zhivago* is playing today."

Nina fought a groan.

What did it say about you when your seventy-year-old grandmother had a more interesting sex life than you did?

Then again, that wasn't entirely true. Not anymore.

The problem lay in that Nina wanted it to continue.

And that the two men involved wanted to make sure it didn't.

Which made her think of another deal.

What if… She wondered. What if she asked them if she could have one more night?

9

LATER THAT NIGHT, Nina sat in the corner of the old neighborhood bar, an umbrella drink untouched on the small table in front of her. The table was meant for two but she was alone. Although she hoped she wasn't going to be that way for long.

She'd arrived fifteen minutes before the band was due to take the stage. The Fantasy Band was mostly made up of local talent, both of the temporary and longstanding kind. The temporary member being Gauge, who was sitting in for the lead guitarist while he was off on his honeymoon with his new wife.

Nina caught movement on the small stage situated beyond the slightly larger dance floor in front of it. The tables were packed, and she craned her neck to see through the crowd. There was Gauge now, putting his guitar strap over his shoulder. He was wearing his usual jeans and dark T-shirt, this one bearing Aerosmith's winged logo. His dark hair was tousled and he smiled at someone in the audience as he gave his instrument a final tuning.

Okay, there was one....

Nina sipped at the sweet concoction in her glass and looked in the other direction, seeking out Kevin. She knew he was coming. Gauge had invited them both earlier in the day. Kevin hadn't committed until after Nina had said she couldn't make it, but had immediatcly said he'd be there when he'd learned she wouldn't be going.

All part of her strategy.

There. There he was. Near the end of the bar wearing his telltale denim shirt over a white T-shirt, one hiking boot on top of the footrest as he accepted a draught beer from the bartender.

Nina smiled. The men were good about banding together at work and providing a united front whenever she approached them. So good, in fact, that she'd given up. Or at least pretended to. She thought that maybe she stood a better chance after they'd both had a beer or two in them...and were away from each other.

Yes, she'd considered going to each of their places alone late at night. Had even driven to Kevin's once…only to be disappointed to find him not home. She'd sat outside his late parents' old Victorian house and waited for a while, but had finally given up without driving by Gauge's apartment building on the outskirts of town.

But tonight…

She caught herself sipping her drink again and pushed it slightly away, already beginning to feel the effects of the disguised alcohol. She grimaced. It wouldn't do her any good at all to get drunk herself. She needed her wits about her if she was going to figure this one out.

"Good evening, everyone," the lead singer of the band said into the mike, indicating that the first set was about to begin.

Nina turned back to face the stage.

"Sitting in for Preston tonight is Patrick Gauge on lead. And he's going to kick things off…."

There was a smattering of applause, but mostly the patrons seemed more interested in getting their buzz on first.

Nina propped her elbow onto the table and rested her chin on the shelf of her hand as the band led into an old rock tune.

Oh, sure, she'd heard Gauge sing before. While he'd never been a lead singer, he could croon a tune along with the best of them. The sexier and bluesier the better. She sighed as he launched into the first line, earning a few hoots and hollers from the single women in the room.

Nina sighed, watching as he came to life under the dim spotlight, his eyes seeming to rest on every person in the place even as he strummed his guitar.

She turned to see what Kevin was doing. She wasn't surprised when she found him looking at her.

She smiled and waved to him, indicating he should join her.

He turned back toward the bar as if pretending he hadn't seen her.

Huh.

Okay, then. If that's the way he wanted to play it.

Since Gauge was occupied on stage, she gathered that there was no time like the present to begin implementing her latest plan.

She rose and picked up her purse and drink, aware of the looks she received from nearby patrons as she edged through the cramped interior. Her clinging, deep-necked black top, and hip-hugging jeans had been designed for a night out such as this.

She reached the bar and elbowed her way in between Kevin and another guy.

"Pardon me," she said with a smile.

The guy gave her a long look. "Anytime, sunshine."

She put her drink on the bar next to Kevin's beer. "I changed my mind," she said to him. "And decided to come."

Kevin grimaced. "So I noticed."

Not that you could tell. He appeared to be going out of his way to keep from looking at her.

"He's doing great, huh?" she said over the sound of the band.

"Who?"

She squinted at him and pointed her thumb over her shoulder in the direction of the band. "Gauge."

"Oh. Yeah."

She pretended to look around. "Did you bring a date?"

He glowered at her, looking even more handsome. "What do you think?"

"I think you came alone."

He took a long pull from his beer and then

grimaced as if he hadn't meant to take such a big sip. She could relate. Her froufrou drink glass was almost empty.

"Can I get you another?" the server asked her.

She felt Kevin's gaze on her as she pushed the glass away. She'd been about to tell him no, but figured she'd probably tip her hand if she did. "Sure. Hit me again."

She looked to see Kevin smiling.

"What?" she asked.

He shook his head. "Nothing. But you might want to take it easy with those."

"It's my third, so what do you know?"

"It's your second and you're not a drinker. And I know a lot about you."

She turned so she was facing him more directly. "Oh, yeah? Like how much?"

His smile vanished.

"Come on, Kevin. You might as well just give up and tell me. I mean, it's not like I'm not going to find out, anyway. Sooner or later, someone's going to give."

"What makes you think it's going to be me? And that it's going to be now?"

She accepted the fresh drink from the server and slowly sipped, using the red straw. She noticed the way Kevin watched her before he forced his gaze away. "You do," she finally said.

"Well, then, I'd have to say you'd be wrong."

She turned more toward the bar. "How'd the game go yesterday, by the way?"

He blinked at her.

"The hockey game? Did your kids win?"

He rubbed the back of his neck. "No, unfortunately we lost. Two-one."

"Sorry to hear that."

"Thanks."

"Sounds like maybe your mind's not on the game."

A male voice sounded behind her. "Nina?"

Damn. She hadn't taken into consideration that a public place meant that people might approach her. While it had been six months since she'd dumped...er, told Paul Jenkins that it might be better if they saw other people, he acted as though it was just yesterday.

"Hi, Paul," she said, unable to bring herself to be rude to the guy. After all, they had been involved for half a year.

"What a pleasure," he said. "Seeing you out."

She wished she could say the same.

"Hey, Kevin," he said.

Kevin returned the greeting and then muttered something under his breath and turned away.

Nina turned away, as well.

But Paul refused to be spurned so easily.

"Hey, you know, seeing you again makes me think of all the good times we used to have." He pushed his eyeglasses up, looking like a younger Mr. Magoo. Nina couldn't imagine what she'd ever seen in him.

Oh, yeah. Sex.

She looked him over.

She must have been really desperate.

Especially considering that she now knew the difference between mediocre, blink-and-it-was-over sex, and all-night-long, hot, crazy sex.

She glanced back toward Kevin, sizing him up.

Paul edged his way around her and in between them, righting his glasses again.

"Anyway, I was thinking that maybe you'd like to dance, you know, during the next slow song. For old times' sake."

Kevin hiked a brow at her over Paul's head. She hadn't realized how tall he was until that moment.

She smiled into her drink. "Sorry, Paul, but I don't think so."

"Oh," he said.

She refused to look at him because she was too afraid she'd feel sorry for the guy and give him a pity dance. That might lead to pity something else. And that was the last thing she wanted just then.

She had bigger fish to fry.

She remembered the other night and swallowed hard.

Much bigger, um, fish.

Kevin cleared his throat and Paul blinked at him as if just realizing he was still there.

"Oh. Okay, then. Maybe some other time."

Nina didn't respond as Paul finally took the hint and left.

"Not again in this lifetime," Kevin said under his breath. "Moron."

Nina laughed, for a moment feeling as if things had gone back to normal.

She tilted her head slightly as she considered her longtime friend. Only they hadn't, though, had they? They could never really return to old times. Not after the other night.

Kevin's grin slowly disappeared again as he took in her thoughtful expression.

He held up a hand to ward off her next attack.

"I'm not going to say a word, Nin, so you might as well give up now."

"What if I told you that I intend never to give up?"

"Then I'd have to say that what I was afraid would happen has."

"What do you mean?"

"That the very framework of the friendship between the three of us has been destroyed."

That hit her where she lived. Nina felt as if someone had just hit her in the chest with a two-by-four.

How far was she really willing to go in her desire to repeat the one hot night? Was she willing to risk their friendship, as Kevin was implying might happen?

She stared down into her frothy drink, her throat too tight to attempt to drink any of it.

Out of the corner of her eye, she watched Kevin peel off a few bills from his wallet and put them on the bar under his empty glass. "This is for the lady's, too," he called out.

The bartender indicated he'd heard.

"I'd better go," he said quietly, moving to step away from the bar then seeming to hesitate.

Nina looked up at him. She wasn't sure what

must have registered on her face—sadness, maybe? Perhaps longing?—but whatever it was had stopped Kevin from leaving as quickly as he apparently wanted to.

"Look, Nina, I'm not doing this to be cruel."

He ran his fingers through his dark hair, tousling it much the same way that Gauge's was on stage. They both had the same type of hair, the same cut. The color was different, but she wouldn't have been able to tell that through feeling it.

"What say we just leave well enough alone, okay? I mean, you enjoyed yourself, didn't you?"

She looked down at her drink again and nodded, fighting the urge to turn the question back around on him.

"So that's it, then?" she asked.

"That was the deal."

"But what if I wanted to alter the deal?"

She peeked to see him narrowing his eyes.

She straightened her shoulders. "What if I decided I wanted another night?"

She'd rendered him speechless....

10

GAUGE WATCHED as Kevin paced back and forth across his apartment later that night. The place was small and cramped, but suited Gauge just fine. Small and cramped was all he needed. So long as there was enough space for a bed and for him to play his guitar, that was all he required.

"She wants another night," Kevin said finally, spilling what was on his mind.

Gauge lay his guitar case on his unmade bed and opened the top, easily pulling the instrument out and placing it on a stand. He could count on one hand how many times Kevin had been at his place. Hell, he hadn't been to Kevin's place all that often, either. He figured it was because they all saw each other enough at work.

That and he was sure that his laid-back environs made the other man itch. While Kevin's uptight house, still boasting framed photos of him growing up along the staircase, and his mother's bovine knickknacks in a glass case in the living room, made Gauge want to jump out of his skin.

"Who wants another night?" he pretended to play dumb.

At least Kevin stopped pacing.

Truth was, all night Gauge had watched his friend stand with Nina at the bar, laughing and talking and ignoring the band and the rest of the patrons.

"Come on, Kev, we've talked about this. We knew she'd try to alter the deal. It's just the way she's made. And it's the entire reason we came up with this to begin with. I mean, if she were capable of rational decisions once she slept with a guy, then we would never have proposed what we did."

Kevin looked like hell warmed over. He'd run his hands through his hair so many times he'd probably pulled a good half of it out. And it appeared as if he hadn't gotten more than two hours' sleep at any one stretch over the past few days.

Gauge sat down on the edge of the bed and pulled his guitar to his knee. Even though he'd played pretty much the entire night, there was something about the weight of the instrument in his hands that made the night not feel so cold or his bed so empty.

Of course, it would have been better if a willing female were there, but in her absence, his guitar was the next best thing.

"How can you be so nonchalant about this?" Kevin asked, finally sitting down in the single ladder-back chair in the corner.

Gauge strummed a few chords of Clapton's "Layla." "How can you be so serious?"

What he was leaving out was that *nonchalant* was his middle name, while *serious* could precede Kevin's name. Serious Kevin. But truth was Gauge was tired of this. And was now questioning the intelligence of having gone through with their plan.

"Look, Kevin, I understand that this is taking a little longer for her to get over. I expected her to give up two days in. But she hasn't." He spun his guitar and put it back on the rack, clenching his hands between his knees. Tonight he could have had his pick of who to bring back to his apartment. And at least three of the women would have been a welcome, if temporary, addition. But he hadn't been interested.

"Can I get you a beer?" he asked as he pushed from the bed.

"No. Thanks."

Gauge stepped to the small kitchen off the main room and opened the refrigerator. As custom dictated, he considered the old appliance's meager offerings. Leftover pizza still in the box that had been there Lord knew how long. A carton of moo-shoo pork. A milk bottle that boasted maybe a swallow that might choke him. And beer.

He grabbed a bottle and popped the top on the lip of the counter.

"So you think she's mistaking sex for a relationship again."

Kevin had followed him into the small room and leaned against the counter, his arms crossed over his chest. Gauge took a deep pull from the bottle and wiped his mouth with the back of his hand. "I'm saying that I'm almost afraid it's going to take her six months to get over a one-night stand."

Kevin flinched.

"Come on, Kev, both you and I know that's all it was. A one-night stand designed to keep her from mistaking sex for a relationship. You should be the last one who's surprised that she's asking for another night. We've both watched her over the past three years. Studied her cycles."

Kevin opened the refrigerator door, considered the contents much as Gauge had, grimaced and then grabbed a beer, as well. He looked around in the drawers for an opener before Gauge took the bottle from him and opened it in the same way and handed it back.

"So what do you suggest we do then?"

"Exactly what we have been doing: stonewalling her."

"She's making that awfully hard."

Gauge nodded. That she was.

Since she was having a hard time figuring out which one of them she'd slept with, not a moment went by when she didn't take full advantage of an opportunity to openly flirt with each of them, trying to get them to tell her. It was enough to make a guy crazy with lust—all that lip-licking and ass-swaying.

He swallowed hard and then took another sip of beer.

Seemed he'd grossly underestimated her talent for seduction. While he'd found himself idly attracted to her before, all he'd had to do before was remind himself of their friendship to cool the flames. Now…

Now he spent every waking moment in a state of near arousal watching her plan her next move.

"And keeping busy," Gauge added.

Kevin frowned. "Hard to do when you work together."

"Tell me about it."

They stood in silence for a few minutes, nothing but the sound of the heat switching on to remind them that life went on around them as usual even if their lives had been turned to utter chaos.

"Maybe what's needed here is a reminder that even if she doesn't take our arrangement seriously, we do."

"How do you mean?"

Gauge shrugged. "I don't know. Maybe a double date would do the trick."

"What?"

He finished his beer and pushed from the wall, dropping the bottle into the garbage bin. "You and me find a couple of women to go out with on a double date. Make sure she sees us. Maybe even introduce her to them. And we leave. Maybe that would make her cool her heels."

Kevin sighed. "She'd see through that in a minute."

"Maybe. Maybe not. You're forgetting, she's allowed her emotions to become involved. She won't be thinking clearly. She may accept the dates for what they are: dates."

"In your case, yes. But in mine?"

"Well, if she thinks you're the one, then she'll know you're capable of great, anonymous sex."

"And if she thinks you're the one?"

Gauge grinned. "She already knows that I'll nail anything that winks at me."

Kevin chuckled. "Cute."

"Ain't it?"

Again, silence.

Gauge had hoped his suggestion would help allay his friend's concerns. But Kevin's wrinkled brow told him he was still working through a few things.

"And if she's hurt?"

"She'll get over it. She always does."

"Does she? Because from what I understand, she's the one used to doing the dumping."

"Kevin, there is no dumping to be done because there was no loading to begin with. It was a one-night stand. Period. Exclamation point. Got it?"

Kevin nodded as if he understood that, yet glared at Gauge as if he was a blink away from blindsiding him with a hard right.

Gauge took the barely touched beer from him, put it on the counter, then grasped him by the shoulder and led him toward the door. "Now go home and get some sleep."

"I wish it were as simple as that."

Gauge felt the same way. Because if he had one more dream about Nina…

He felt Kevin's gaze on him and grinned. "It will be if you let it be."

"Is everything always so simple to you?" Gauge detected more than a hint of acid in his friend's voice.

"No. But I try to make it simple. Complicated…well, complicated is complicated. And messy."

He pushed him through the door.

"Goodnight, Kevin."

"Goodnight, Gauge."

Gauge stood for a long moment watching as his friend shrugged back into his coat and walked toward his car before he finally closed the door.

"Time has come to move on," he heard his old man's voice in his head.

Gauge ran his hand over his face, cringing at the scratching of his stubble against his palm.

"Done worn out our welcome in another town."

His young life had been full of similar such declarations. Sometimes it took a month. Sometimes three. Then there were other times when only a day was needed before Gauge was packing the truck again and he and his dad were rolling on down the road to the next stop.

Maybe the time had, indeed, come again....

NINA RESET the treadmill to a lower speed, sweat dripping from every pore as a result of her running for the past twenty minutes straight. No jogging. Running, flat out.

"Hey, what are you trying to get away from?" one of the girls working out next to her had asked ten minutes in.

She'd smiled at her and then kept her gaze forward.

It wasn't so much what she was running from, but what she was running toward.

More specifically, she needed completion on this entire matter before she went postal. And the only thing capable of keeping her mind off Kevin and Gauge was a good visit to the gym.

So she'd gone to the gym on her dinner break, trying to ban her conversation with Kevin at the bar last night and the day full of unanswered questions from her mind.

This was driving her nuts.

Especially since both Gauge and Kevin were now openly going out of their way to avoid her at every turn.

In the beginning they'd been a little subtler about it.

Now, when she entered their sections of the store, they made a beeline for another area, or approached a customer, or took some other sort of evasive action that sent her straight back to the café.

Judging that she'd cooled down enough, she grabbed her towel from the handle and shut down the treadmill, wiping the sweat from her face. She'd had much more alcohol to drink than she'd planned at the bar and now she shook her water bottle to find it empty. She filled it at the water fountain before she headed for the showers, drinking as she went.

It was after nine and the place had pretty much emptied out while she ran. She liked it like that. She wouldn't be required to make conversation with anyone and thus wouldn't be at risk of blurting out her current dilemma.

She inwardly groaned and she took another deep drink from her water bottle and then began stripping out of her shorts and T-shirt as soon as the locker-room door closed behind her.

She could just imagine the small town's reaction to the news that she secretly fantasized about sleeping with her two business partners, and that the other night they'd redefined the meaning of "best" friends. BMC would go out of business overnight. And something similar to the letter *S* would be stamped across the front window, labeling them all as sinners.

But they weren't really sinners, were they? Okay, so she didn't know which man she'd slept with, but they were all three friends and she knew it was one or the other of them. There was nothing wrong with sleeping with one of your friends, was there?

Another twenty minutes later she was back at her place, showered and sitting at her kitchen table eating a bowl of granola even as Ernie crunched on his food nearby. But her mind wasn't on the food or her cat. Instead, she was thinking about the shop's parking lot and the fact that Kevin's car was gone while Gauge's car still there.

Her chewing slowed. Was that music she heard?

Her apartment sat over the music center, Gauge's area of the shop. And while it wasn't unusual to hear strains of whatever new CD he'd gotten in, she seemed especially tuned in to the sounds now.

Only it wasn't a CD, was it? Rather, she heard only a guitar. His guitar, she suspected.

She shivered and tossed the remainder of her cereal then stared down at Ernie who had finished eating and sat staring up at her.

"What?" she whispered. "I'm not thinking of doing anything stupid."

He flicked his tail as if to say, "Yeah, right," and then left the room, probably to find a safe spot that wouldn't result in him being locked in the kitchen again.

11

GAUGE SAT on a stool in the back area of the music section, trying to show nineteen-year-old Sasha Haskins how to get over her fear of pain as she ran her delicate fingertips over the unforgiving guitar strings.

Nineteen. Young. Pretty. And she smelled like magnolias, reminding him of Memphis and hot summer nights.

He knew that Sasha's interest in taking guitar lessons had as much to do with him as with any true interest in music. She'd been sitting at the front tables sipping soda when he played at Henry's lately. And she'd dropped a fortune on CDs in the past couple of months, finding some reason to speak to him about this band or that. He'd sucked up the attention, much as he did with every interested, beautiful woman that crossed his path.

Then, earlier today she'd asked him what he thought her mother might like for her birthday since he was around the same age and any amorous moves he might have made on her flew right out the door with her when she finally left. Especially when he realized that he knew her mother and he'd thought himself at least a decade younger than her.

And perhaps he was. But that didn't change the fact that Sasha, however innocently, had put him in the same category as her mother.

"Don't shy away from it, Sasha," he said quietly as she barely made a C-note.

He put his own guitar down and moved to stand behind her, stretching his left arm the length of hers. It was a move he'd made at least a thousand time during lessons. But now he was overly aware of how close he was to his student.

He left his right hand at his side and pressed his fingers against the tops of hers, forcing the pads of her fingers against the strings.

"Ow," she said, but didn't jerk away from him.

Damn, but she smelled good. "Only practice and time will help you develop the calluses you need so it won't hurt," he told her. "See mine?"

He held his left hand in front of her. She

leaned the guitar against her chest and used both her hands to examine his one. The way she poked and probed his skin made him think of a palm reader. But he didn't think she was interested in how long his lifeline was.

The quietness of the shop amplified the sound of footsteps in the apartment above the shop. Nina's apartment, indicating she'd probably returned home from somewhere.

Gauge grimaced and withdrew his hand.

"I think that's enough for today, Sasha. Why don't you go on home and practice."

"But I still have fifteen minutes to go in the lesson."

"Yes, well, we got a late start. And, anyway, until you learn how to play the simple chords I gave you three lessons ago, we don't have anywhere else to go."

It wasn't like him to be short with a customer. But, damn it, Nina and this whole situation was driving him to distraction.

And having nineteen-year-old flirty beauties who used to make up the bulk of his mainstay mention their mothers' names in the same sentence with his might be a little to blame for throwing him off his game.

He returned to the cashier's station and made a notation in the appointment book.

"I'll discount today's lesson, how's that?" he asked Sasha as she shrugged into her coat and then hoisted up her guitar case even though she'd been the one who was almost an hour late.

He followed her to the door, idly watching the way her jeans fitted as he let her out the front door.

"Thanks, Gauge. Same time on Thursday?"

"See you then."

He closed the door and locked it and then turned around and leaned against the cold glass, considering the quiet store around him.

Kevin had had hockey practice tonight and a dinner with his late mother's friends after that, having left the shop a good three hours ago.

He knew he should probably follow suit, maybe head down to the bar where someone else was sitting in with the band tonight, but instead he found his feet leading him back to the music center. He put away the music he'd opened on the stand, repositioned the screen for privacy and then slid a Stevie Ray Vaughan CD into the player, turning the volume to low before taking his chair behind the screen. He positioned the guitar in his hands and closed his eyes, feeling at once at peace with the instrument.

And then he began playing.

There was a time not so long ago when he'd imagined music playing the starring role in his life. Traveling. Playing in bands. Perhaps in search of that elusive lucrative contract that would net him countless acres of prime real estate in Southern California.

What he hadn't factored into that vision was a small town called Fantasy and two important people he called friends.

Friends.

His right hand strummed the strings with more force.

Growing up, he hadn't had much of an opportunity to explore the meaning of words like *friend* or *home* or *family*. Oh, he'd had his father. At least until he'd essentially drunk himself to death when Gauge was sixteen, his life ending in one of the countless ratty motel rooms they'd stayed in across the country, one no different from the rest. They'd been on the outskirts of St. Louis and it was there that Gauge had buried his father in a small church plot. He and an aging waitress his father had spent the night with before he died attended the burial service.

Then Gauge had moved on. Leading the only life he'd known how to live, driving the beat-up pickup truck—the only thing his father had left him aside from a battered old suitcase of clothes and a guitar—from place to place, town to town, picking up money from playing in bars either as a solo act or part of an already established band. And taking loving anywhere he could get it, leaving the women behind when it was time to move on.

"What's that?"

The words behind him caused his hands to slow but not stop. He hadn't expected Nina to come downstairs. But at the sound of her soft voice, he realized he'd been hoping she would.

"Stevie Ray Vaughan," he said, sitting with his back to her.

Silence. And then, "I like it."

Gauge continued playing, sensitively aware of her standing behind him.

Until he heard her move….

IT WAS Gauge.

Nina was sure of that now. Hadn't known how

she'd missed the signs. Gauge was bold and ex-plorative. He would take what he wanted and make sure she had a good time in the process. The things he'd done…she shivered. The things he'd done were the mark of an experienced man. A man who'd been around more than a few women and knew what pleased them.

It was gratifying to have the mystery finally solved. To know the identity of the man who had brought her so much pleasure. Who had opened her closed eyes to a world of sensations she hadn't known existed.

She moved slowly forward, surprisingly shy without the blindfold. But not so shy that she hadn't come down in only her white silk robe. Her feet were bare against the wood floor and she half wished he'd been sitting in the main store where the fireplace could have been lit.

Then again, in the main bookstore, they would have been visible from the outside.

Here…

The music center was protected by prying eyes by the CD posters that plastered the front windows to ward off direct sunlight. Gauge called it ambience.

Right now it afforded privacy.

Nina drew even with Gauge, finding his eyes closed, his hands sliding knowingly over the guitar strings with beautiful precision. He was a poet, music maker and lover in one. She'd watched him pull songs out of thin air as if he were doing little more than catching a firefly. Witnessed his trancelike state when he was playing…much like the one he was in now.

She kept moving until she stood a few feet in front of him, waiting for him to notice her.

She'd been in this section of the store countless times. This is where they hosted author signings, where Gauge taught guitar lessons, and where Saturday afternoon story sessions were held.

But now, at night, with the lights down low, and with no one around, it seemed completely different. Foreign. Comfortable. It was set up to resemble someone's study with a long leather couch and matching chairs, a low-lying coffee table holding CDs and books and coupons for the café.

The guitar playing stopped. Nina blinked to find that Gauge had finally opened his eyes and sat looking at the front of her robe as if he'd seen a ghost.

She smiled. "I couldn't sleep."

He swallowed thickly.

She noticed that he didn't bother to deny that he'd been her mysterious lover.

She ran her fingertips along the inside flap of her robe, then reached down and untied the belt, allowing the sleek silk to fall open and reveal that she wore nothing underneath.

"Nina...."

"Shhh," she said, stepping closer to him, watching as his pupils dilated, the black nearly taking over the gray of his eyes. "No words. Please."

She reached for his guitar and easily put it in its stand and then moved into the V of his knees, putting her breasts directly in front of his face.

He groaned and slid his hands inside her robe, grasping her hips even as he pressed his mouth against the skin between her breasts.

Nina caught her breath, the feel of his hands and his mouth robbing her of air.

Ever since that night she'd dreamed of this moment when she might reclaim what had been freely given and then taken from her again. She'd thought about all the things they'd done, and those that they hadn't, planning to rectify that the next go around.

And now the next time stretched wickedly in front of her.

She threaded her fingers through his hair even as he nudged the flap of her robe until it fell on the other side of her breast, baring her nipple. A nipple he claimed in his mouth, drawing deeply.

A hot, liquid heat pooled in her belly.

She didn't know where they would go from there. If, indeed, they would go anywhere. All she knew was that she wanted this, wanted this one moment, even if it was to be only one moment.

She knew Gauge wasn't a man given to commitment. But in their time together he'd given her something no one else had. Introduced her to different levels of sensation that she'd never experienced. And so long as he agreed to indulge her, she intended to take advantage of his attentions. Explore the new emotions and pursue them to their natural end, common sense be damned.

He switched his attention to her other breast and she moved her torso closer until she leaned her bare womanhood against the cotton of his T-shirt. Despite the cool air, she felt hot. Unbearably hot.

And he emerged the one man capable of fanning and then dousing the flames that licked over her skin.

His hands slid from her hips, curving back over her bottom and down until he firmly gripped her. Nina gasped when he pressed her even more fully against him, causing her pulse to throb between her legs.

Oh, yes....

12

NINA HAD BEGUN to fear she'd never feel this way again. Never experience this exquisite longing. Revel in pure, sweet wanton desire.

Gauge worked one of his knees between hers, parting her, baring her most intimate parts to his heated gaze.

"Condom," she whispered.

"Not yet."

She shuddered at the thought of what he planned to do to her in plain sight. It was one thing to have him plunder and explore from behind the safety of a blindfold…quite another to watch a man she'd known for the past three years touch her in a way few others had.

He put his hands together, palm to palm, and then slid them between her thighs. The shivering began in Nina's toes and worked its way up until her very hair trembled in anticipation.

FREE BOOKS OFFER

To get you started, we'll send you
2 FREE books and a FREE gift

There's no catch, everything is **FREE**

Accepting your 2 **FREE** books and **FREE** mystery gift
places you under no obligation to buy anything.

Be part of the Mills & Boon® Book Club™ and receive your favourite
Series books up to 2 months before they are in the shops and delivered
straight to your door. Plus, enjoy a wide range of **EXCLUSIVE** benefits!

- Best new women's fiction – delivered right to
  your door with FREE P&P

- Avoid disappointment – get your books up to
  2 months before they are in the shops

- No contract – no obligation to buy

We hope that after receiving your free books you'll
want to remain a member. But the choice is yours.
So why not give us a go? You'll be glad you did!

Visit **millsandboon.co.uk** to stay up to date
with offers and to sign-up for our newsletter

2 **FREE** books
and a
FREE gift

NO STAMP
NEEDED!

MILLS & BOON®
Book Club

FREE BOOK OFFER
FREEPOST CN81
CROYDON
CR9 3WZ

NO STAMP
NECESSARY
IF POSTED IN
THE U.K. OR N.I.

Gauge nudged his hands upward, teasing her skin with the back of his knuckles as he moved.

Nina swallowed thickly, not knowing what was expected of her, if, indeed, anything was.

The other night she'd had no other choice but to stand and wait for him to initiate action. But now she was free to roam with her hands and her eyes. Only the view was somehow too intimate, too carnal, and she found herself closing her eyes.

"No, Nina," he whispered. "I want you to watch me make love to you."

The words finished at the same time his hands met her tingling flesh and his thumbs moved to part her swollen womanhood and find her tight bud.

Nina threw her head back and moaned. So hot. Then forced herself to do as he asked and watched him through hooded eyes, her breath coming in rapid gasps. Gauge leaned forward, running his tongue along her throbbing clit, and then leaned back and blew.

And she exploded into a million crystalline pieces right there in the middle of the store.

WOMEN HAD always fascinated Gauge. One touch, one caress, placed just so and they melted in your hand.

His first sexual experience had come when he was thirteen and had been with one of the women his father had brought back to the motel room. He'd gone into the bathroom in the morning to find the young woman in the shower. He'd begun to back out, apologizing, but she told him she didn't mind. And he'd gotten the distinct impression that not only hadn't she minded, but that she enjoyed his wide-eyed attention.

Oh, he'd known about the birds and the bees for a long time. It was hard not to when he shared a room with his father who brought home a different woman every other night and had his way with her in the bed a few feet away from Gauge's own. But while he might have caught a glimpse of bare flesh in the shadows, this open display of being invited to watch in the plain light of day had been a first.

And he'd taken full advantage of it.

Especially when she'd opened the shower curtain and invited him to join her, taking some sort of odd pleasure in being the one to bust his cherry, as she'd put it.

The experience hadn't lasted long. But it had been enough for him to know that he wanted more. Much more.

And he'd gotten it. First from a few of his father's women…then from his own.

Then there was Nina….

He ran his tongue the length of Nina's tight bud and then blew on the closed blossom, sitting back to watch as she bloomed.

He'd somehow never expected her to be so responsive…so uninhibited. He touched her and she trembled with anticipation. It was enough to send a man sailing over the edge without being touched himself.

Oh, but he definitely intended to be touched.

Somewhere in the back of his mind he heard the store phone ring, but he was too far gone to give it more than a passing notice. It was past closing time. Probably a wrong number.

Nina had grasped on to his shoulders during orgasm and now smiled down at him, her face a portrait of bliss. He groaned and reached for the condom she had asked for moments before even as she popped the front of his jeans.

The urgency that filled him wouldn't allow for any prolonged foreplay. He brushed her hands away when she reached to touch him, and sheathed himself, grabbing only a breath before positioning her legs on the outside of his and then tugging her down so that her silk heat lay against his erection. He grasped her hips, watching her face, licking her firm, high breasts. She tasted as good as she looked.

Before he was ready, she slid down over his length to the hilt, taking in every inch of him, her body shivering in response.

Dear Lord, she was going to be the end of him.

"Yes." The single word came out as a hushed whisper from her pink lips.

She slid slowly up and then came back down again, her velvet muscles squeezing each time her sweet ass touched his thighs. He loosened the arms she had tightened around his neck and coaxed her to lean back so he could view where their bodies met. His erection glistened from her hot juices as she lifted herself again, then it disappeared into her bared flesh.

Gauge gritted his teeth to fight off ejaculation. He hadn't felt this way since that first time in the shower when he was thirteen. His balls ached with the urgent need to spill his seed. His heart beat so hard in his chest all he could hear was the sound of it and his own ragged breathing.

He trapped one of her breasts in his hand and

covered the tip in his mouth, swirling his tongue around the distended tip, then sucking deeply. She moaned, her slow, sexy movements as she rode him stuttering slightly with the dual assault.

He looked into her passion-clouded blue eyes and something stabbed him deep in his gut, a feeling that quickly passed as she slid down him again.

Clenching his teeth together, he grasped her hips and lifted her from him because if he didn't he was afraid it would be over before it had begun.

She reluctantly rose to her feet, and he followed, stepping out of his boots, jeans and T-shirt as he led her toward the couch. She began to lie down faceup and he caught her, instead turning her so that she knelt on the seat facing away from him. She instantly grasped the back to balance herself and arched her spine, bringing her sweet ass up to greet him.

Christ, but she was sexy. Her womanhood was engorged and full, her inner lips pink and inviting. He grabbed his erection and guided the head to rest against her tight portal. She moaned, bearing back against him. He stayed her with a hand against her lower back, holding her there as he entered her a couple of inches and then withdrew. And then entered her again, and again, each time going a little deeper, but stopping himself from going in to the hilt.

Her shallow breaths filled his ears as she restlessly flicked her blond hair over one shoulder, trying to see him before moaning and dropping her head to the back of the leather couch. Her pink-tipped fingers tightly grasped the cushions.

Finally he slid into her fully in one, smooth move.

Her long, low moan swirled around him, nearly bringing him to climax.

He tightened his muscles and briefly closed his eyes, ordering his body to obey him.

Once he'd recovered a modicum of control, he began stroking her with his rigid member, in and out, slowly increasing the frequency of his thrusts until flesh slapped against flesh.

When he was about to race right over the cliff's edge, he completely withdrew, denying not only her, but himself as he fought to catch his breath.

"Please…please," she whimpered, her hands blindly reaching for him to coax him to reenter her.

He became aware of the picture they made, the two of them in a public area of the store past closing time, cloaked by night, but not completely. If someone looked just the right way from the front windows, they'd be able to see a carnal view of them both naked, him taking Nina from behind.

And he wanted everyone to see....

IT WAS almost midnight and the air was cold, the wind chill hovering somewhere just below zero. Kevin parked his car, noting that Nina's Honda was there in the lot, along with Gauge's Chevy.

That was funny. Why wouldn't either one of them answer their phones?

He walked to the back door of the shop, taking his keys from his pocket as he went. But he didn't need them. It was unlocked.

He stepped inside the storeroom and shook off the cold. He didn't like being the bearer of bad news. But this was the type of thing that couldn't hold until morning.

He was only glad he wouldn't have to go looking for Nina around town. He'd check in with Gauge and then head upstairs. Or perhaps Gauge could do it. He didn't want to have to go up to her apartment again unless he absolutely had to.

He navigated his way through the bookstore,

familiar with every nook and cranny and title that graced the floor-to-ceiling shelves. As he should be. He'd created them.

He shrugged out of his coat and laid it on the counter even as he headed in the direction of the music center. He tilted his head, listening for sounds. He made out the low whine of an electric guitar on a blues track. Clapton? He couldn't be sure.

He stepped into the area and looked around, not immediately seeing anyone or anything. Where was Gauge?

He leaned over the counter. The register was closed and locked. He rounded it, nearing the door to the café. The lights were off in there, and he couldn't make out the smell of any cooking. Not that he expected to. Nina had left before he had.

That was strange. He'd come in through the storage room and no one had been in there….

A sound caught his attention behind him, causing the fine hair on the back of his neck to stand on end. He cocked his head, listening.

There. There it was again. The sound of a woman moaning, in the throes of passion.

He grimaced and smoothed his hand over the back of his neck. Had Gauge brought a woman in here? While he hadn't known his friend ever to do anything like that before, he wouldn't put it past him. How many times had Gauge commented that he'd like to date one customer or another?

Then again, it was too late for any customers.

His heart pitched to his feet as he heard another moan and the groan of couch springs.

Kevin slowly headed in the direction of the public gathering area, his gaze missing the carefully hand-painted graffiti-style butterflies on the screen that afforded privacy but could easily be removed when an author was signing. Dread lined his stomach with each step. He couldn't be sure why.

Until he rounded the screen and saw that Gauge was, indeed, indulging in in-store sex.

Only his partner wasn't one of his customers, but Nina....

13

NINA SAW KEVIN first. She was stretching her back to take in more of Gauge one moment, the next she was restlessly trying to see him…and saw Kevin standing a few feet away instead.

She wasn't sure what tipped her off, but in that instant she understood one, sad, unavoidable truth: it hadn't been Gauge in her bed that night. It had been Kevin.

Any pleasure she'd been feeling vanished and she moved quickly away from the man even now searching for climax, folding in on herself as she took in Kevin's shocked expression.

But it was more than shock that made her heart pitch to her feet. It was the pain visible there in his dark eyes.

"You son of a bitch."

The moment she moved away Gauge had turned to see their best friend standing behind him. He reached for his jeans and jerked them on, barely doing up half the buttons before Kevin stepped forward and landed a punch right on his jaw.

Nina scrambled for her robe, quickly putting it on.

"Kevin, no!" She tried to put herself between them. Act as a mediator between the two men who were her best friends, her business partners…her lovers.

"Hey, man, calm down," Gauge said, finding his footing even as he rubbed his jaw, as if checking its integrity.

Kevin's shock and pain had turned to pure anger. Igniting an unfamiliar sadness in Nina's chest.

"Please, Kevin…."

He blinked at her, myriad emotions passing over his face. "Move out of the way, Nina."

"I—I can't," she said, trembling for reasons that had nothing to do with sex and everything to do with fear.

"Hey, Kev, it's not my fault, man," Gauge said.

Nina glanced over her shoulder, trying to tell him to be quiet.

"She came down here in that slinky thing and then opened it to reveal she was nude…." He finished doing up his jeans, put on his boots and then reached for his T-shirt. "I'm only human, man. No red-blooded man would have been able to look that in the eye and turn it down."

Nina didn't know what Gauge had been hoping to achieve, but she guessed it was the exact opposite of what was happening.

She watched Kevin clench and unclench his fists.

"Get out of the way, Nina," he said again.

"Kevin, don't," she whispered, tears burning her eyes. She laid her hands against his chest. She felt like her heart was being ripped from her chest.

How could this have happened? How could she have mistaken Gauge for Kevin?

She didn't have time to further contemplate the question as Kevin physically moved her aside and fell on Gauge like a ton of angry bricks.

Nina stared helplessly as the two men fought in front of her. At first Gauge straightened his shoulders and took Kevin's hits, almost as if he felt he deserved them. Then Kevin landed a punch straight on his nose. He lifted a hand to find blood trailing down, and his stance changed to allow him to confront the man by assaulting him, head-on.

Nina gasped as the two men fell to the floor, rolling over and over again as one and then the other tried to gain the upper hand.

What should she do? Should she call the sheriff? Call for help? Surely if they continued like this someone would get seriously hurt.

"Stop!" she shouted, grabbing the back of Kevin's shirt as he sat on top of Gauge. "Oh, God, please stop!"

Her words finally appeared to register as Kevin looked at her, emerging from his blind rage and focusing on her tear-streaked face.

"Stop it. Now. Both of you," she said, feeling dangerously close to sobbing.

Kevin was distracted enough to allow Gauge to scoot out from under him. He used a chair to rise to a standing position even as Kevin stood as well. They were both out of breath and bore the signs of their scuffle.

Nina wished she could curl up and disappear as she faced them both, Kevin looking as if she'd buried a ten-inch knife in his back, Gauge with his chin tucked slightly down as he ran his hand across his nose, wiping off the blood there, looking like the kid who had got caught stealing.

Kevin turned and began walking away without a word.

Nina started after him, panic surging through her bloodstream. "Kevin, wait—"

He swung back toward her, looking amazingly close to lifting his hand to her.

Nina froze, her stomach pitching to her feet as she became aware of the dark depths of his pain and anger.

"I almost forgot why I came here," he said, his gaze boring into her. "Your grandmother had a heart attack. When your mother couldn't get hold of you, she tried calling the store and then contacted me." He named a hospital and then went silent.

Nina wished he had slapped her instead of uttering the words he had. At least the sting of the physical attack would have passed.

THE DRIVE into Detroit had seemed to take forever. Nina had turned down Gauge's offer to take her into the city, figuring they had both done enough damage for one night.

As for Kevin…

Her heart lurched and tears rushed her eyes anew.

How had she missed the signs? How had she thought it had been Gauge who had rocked her world when all along it had been quiet Kevin?

She remembered the bold touches, the insatiable edge to their lovemaking. Her mind told her it was only natural that she would think Gauge would be the one behind the moves.

Why, oh why, hadn't he told her? Why had she acted on stupid suppositions tonight?

Why hadn't she allowed Gauge to talk when he'd tried to say something as she'd first opened her robe?

She rapidly blinked her eyes to clear them, the road before her blurring. It was past 1:00 a.m., and she was grateful the Detroit traffic was light. Right after Kevin had shared his reason for showing up at the store, she'd rushed upstairs and called her mother even as she dressed. Helen had told her that Gladys had complained of chest pains during dinner and had shortly thereafter been taken to the hospital. She was stable now, but she was scheduled for surgery first thing in the morning.

She'd wanted to talk to her grandmother, hear for herself that she was okay, but her mother had said she was resting and that she should wait until morning to come in.

But Nina hadn't been able to face the thought of being so far away from her grandmother while she lay in a hospital bed. So she'd gotten into her car and driven until she finally reached the hospital.

Parking in the underground lot, she hurried to the emergency room only to be told that her grandmother had been moved to a private room and that she wouldn't be able to see her until 7:00 a.m.

Nina didn't care. If she had to wait, she had to wait. But at least she felt better knowing that she was only a moment away rather than an hour and a half.

Besides, she didn't think she would have gotten much sleep tonight anyway....

"YOU LOOK as bad as I feel."

Nina sat next to her grandmother's bed. For the past half hour she'd watched her mother fuss over everything, rearranging the ice pitcher and the food tray and the flowers she'd brought. Essentially doing everything but quietly talking to the woman who had raised her.

Nina had watched passively, feeling as bad as her grandmother had suggested she looked after spending a sleepless, tortured night sitting in the waiting room until she'd been allowed to see Gladys.

Finally, her mother had left to go talk to the nurses about bringing in more personal items and whether or not it was okay to bring in her own bedding since these sheets were going to chafe her mother's skin.

And Gladys had turned to Nina the instant the door had closed behind Helen's retreating back.

"Out with it, girl," Gladys said.

Nina gave a watery smile, stroking her grandmother's hand. Her nails were perfectly manicured, bearing scarlet nail polish.

How had she not noticed how old she was before? She lost count of the age spots on Gladys's hand, saw the veins standing in relief against thinning skin. She was sure that the white sheets were somewhat to blame for her paleness, along with her poor condition, but seeing her grandmother lying there looking like a thousand other aging women struck Nina as somehow wrong.

"I'm not here to talk about me. I'm here to talk about you," she said quietly, being careful not to hold her grandmother's gaze for too long for fear that she'd blurt everything out.

She hadn't heard from either Gauge or Kevin all night. Not that she had expected to. But she had hoped one or both of them might call to check up on Gladys's condition and see if she needed anything.

That was exactly what they would have done any other time….

But this wasn't any other time, was it? She'd gone from refusing to have an intimate relationship with either one of them over the past three years, to sleeping with both within the span of a week.

"I'm tired of hearing about me," Gladys said quietly, watching her expressions. "Ever since I got here last night I've been asked the same damn questions by three different doctors. The nurses have been poking holes in my flawless skin. And just what is that smell, anyway?"

"It's called a hospital, Nana."

"Yeah, well," Gladys took her hand from Nina's and smoothed down the blankets Helen had folded perfectly over her stomach. "I don't like it."

"What happened?" Nina asked.

"What do you mean what happened? I had a heart attack, that's what happened."

Nina smiled. "I'm talking about what brought it on."

Gladys gave an eye roll. "Oh, that."

Nina held up her hand. "If you were having sex, I don't think I want to know about it."

She laughed. "Trust me, if I'd been having sex at the time, it's the first thing I'd tell you." Her smile vanished and she frowned. "I was eating goat cheese."

Nina tried to follow her. "You were eating... goat cheese?"

"Yes, damn it. I was eating goat cheese. You know, that stuff they set on fire over in Greek Town? Not doing a back flip in bed or running away from a wild bear. I was sitting in an expensive restaurant waiting to dig in to goat cheese and my heart picked then to give out."

Nina squinted at her. "Define *give out*."

"The damn thing up and decided to quit on me. Right there." She moved her hand to her chest and patted it. "Bub-bub. Bub-bub. Then nothing." She sighed heavily. "I didn't even feel any pain. One minute I was in a chair applauding the waiter. The next I was on the floor and he was giving me mouth-to-mouth."

Nina swallowed hard, envisioning the scene. Her lively grandmother celebrating life one moment, teetering on the edge of death the next.

The idea sent a bolt of fear through her spine.

"The waiter could have been hot, at least," she said. "That would have made the story more interesting. But I think he's one of the owners and he hasn't taken good care of himself and…well, it just would have been more interesting if it had been some other young stud."

"Grandmother!"

"What?" She grinned. "It's true. I'm just calling it as I see it."

"Yes, well, if you'd done a little less of that, maybe you wouldn't be in the mess you're in now."

She was one to talk about messes. In one fell swoop, she'd made a hell of a mess out of her own life, hadn't she? Not only had she probably lost both of her best friends, the very future of their store was on the line.

She groaned inwardly, not capable of thinking about that just then.

"Surely you're not saying I shouldn't live my life as I see fit?"

Nina glanced down to her hands clasped in her lap. "I'm saying that maybe it's time you considered slowing down a bit, Nana." She hated saying the words.

"Now you sound like your mother."

Nina realized that she was right. She did sound like her mother.

But maybe her mother wasn't far off base. Perhaps if she'd lived more as her mother had wanted her to live, and not taken her grandmother's wild life as an example, she wouldn't be going through what she was.

And neither would her grandmother.

Gladys pointed a finger at her and then at herself. "You and me, we need to have a chat." She frowned. "Only I don't think now's the time. Not with your mother due back here in—"

The door opened and Helen breezed back into the room with a fresh blanket and pillow. "Look what I found. They're not much better than what you have, but they'll have to do for now."

Nina shared a long-suffering glance with her grandmother and both of them sat back and allowed Hurricane Helen to dominate the conversation.

Which was just fine with Nina. At least for now. She had quite enough on her plate that minute. And she wasn't ready for her grandmother to start picking over it with her sharp fork.

At least not yet.

14

KEVIN SAT in the kitchen of the house that had been his only home. He hadn't turned up the heat when he came in after closing the store, and the room was chilly. Not that he noticed. And the only light came from the hall. Not that he gave that much attention, either.

A half-full bottle of Jack Daniel's sat on the table at his elbow, along with an empty glass. The bottle had been full when he'd taken it from the cupboard an hour ago.

But no matter how much he tried, he couldn't erase the image of Gauge and Nina together from the back of his eyelids.

He picked up the bottle and poured another finger into the glass and quickly downed the contents. His mouth and throat were already numb from the alcohol. He wished that numbness on the rest of him. His mind would be a good place to start.

And his heart ran a quick second.

He lifted the bottle again and then dropped it back down, liquid sloshing out of the top and splattering against the tabletop.

Outside of the image of Gauge and Nina, everything that had happened since last night merged into a blur. He'd somehow made it home, but he hadn't slept. On autopilot, he'd gone to open the store this morning, feeling strangely disconnected from everything that he did. Gauge was already there when he arrived, but he hadn't even spared his onetime best friend a look, much less acknowledged him when he'd come to his counter and said that they needed to talk.

Kevin had ignored him and he'd gone away. But he didn't kid himself into thinking that that would last long. Gauge would continue to pursue him until he finally gave in. Of that much he was sure.

All day he'd itched to call Nina. To see how her grandmother was doing. To see how she was doing. But every time he thought about it, the slicing pain of betrayal would lance through him and he'd force the idea from his mind.

Her assistant, Heidi, had come in earlier to say that Gladys was recovering and that Nina had asked her to pack a bag for her, that she would be staying in the city for a few days. Heidi had asked him for the key to her place.

He'd been glad that he hadn't had to see to the matter himself. That she hadn't called him and asked him to bring her a bag.

Equally he hated that she hadn't.

He groaned and sank down in the uncomfortable chair, a chair that hadn't been built to be sat in for long periods. Actually, everything in this house seemed to have been built for beauty, for show rather than for comfort. It was a showplace where his mother could entertain and have visitors appreciate the way her Wedgwood china was displayed, or how her collection of Swarovski crystal animal figures shone.

He rubbed his closed eyelids, recalling with vivid clarity his conversation with Gauge an hour before the designated time for someone to meet Nina in her apartment, anonymously.

"You've got to be the biggest sap north of the Ohio border," Gauge had told him. "Admit it, man, you've been in love with the woman since the instant you first set eyes on her. I can see it.

Everyone else but you and Nina can see it. Why don't you just own up to it already?"

Own up to it, indeed.

Kevin had known in that one instant that what Gauge had said was true: he was in love with Nina. Always had been. And probably always would be.

And he'd had that love thrown back into his face, just as he'd feared would happen.

Yes, he'd loved Nina. She was the reason why he couldn't see anyone else beyond a date or two, because inevitably her face would come into focus when any kind of intimacy was expressed, her laughter would echo in his ears, her soft words would tickle his ears.

That one night had seemed like the perfect opportunity to exorcise her once and for all from his heart. No, he could probably never have her in the real world. But in the fantasy world, she would get the anonymous sex she sought and he would get the avenue he needed finally to move beyond his wild infatuation with her.

Only it hadn't worked that way, had it? He'd shown up to find her wearing that silky nightgown while kneeling in the middle of her bed, the black blindfold against her white-blonde hair, and his feelings for her had been amplified.

Sexual desire. That's what he'd put it down to. He'd wanted her for so long, passion was clouding his judgment. But from the moment he first touched her, stroked her slick heat, buried himself deep inside her, he recognized that the love he felt wasn't going to go anywhere. That he had just cemented that she would be the one woman he wanted, but beyond that night, could never have.

So he'd prepared himself to move on. Convinced himself that Gauge was right; if Nina discovered who the stranger was, she'd attach romantic significance to the encounter, and Kevin would find himself thrown to the curb in six months' time, just like every other poor schmoe she'd dated and left.

He couldn't have handled that. Couldn't have loved her for six months only to have her wake up one morning and decide she no longer wanted him.

That's all he had to remind himself of every time she approached him with her sexy smile and suggestive comments designed to draw him out.

"Don't give in, Kev," Gauge had told him. "It's better that she not know who she spent the night with."

"Better for whom?" he'd ground out, going insane with the need to claim her again, even if it was only for a few sweet, short moments.

"Better for you…for her…"

More like it was better for Gauge, Kevin reasoned.

He picked up the bottle to pour some more of the blessed liquid into his glass and then hurled it across the kitchen instead, watching it crash against the wall, throwing shards of glass and whiskey all over the kitchen. He was strangely out of breath and his heart beat as if it might explode straight from his chest.

Never in a million years would he have expected to see the scene laid out in front of him last night. Nina kneeling on the couch, her bottom high in the air while Gauge serviced her from behind.

Kevin got up quickly and grabbed the uncomfortable chair, picking it up and slamming it against the table. It took three times before the sturdy furniture finally gave, splintering into several pieces. He reached for another chair, firmly ignoring the small voice in the back of his head telling him that if he no longer wanted his mother's stuffy, overly ornate furniture, surely a needy family would welcome it.

He didn't care. Not right that moment.

So he spent the next hour smashing everything that could be broken, outside of a few of his mother's most cherished pieces that he could give to his aunt, her sister. He wasn't surprised when he heard the doorbell. He went to answer it, several cuts on his face and arms from where shards had nicked him in his activities, and stood sweating, staring at the young sheriff's deputy.

Bertram had looked him over, taking in his sweaty condition, his ripped and smeared clothing, and his general agitated state that breaking all the furniture in the county would never assuage and asked, "What's going on, Kevin?"

"I'm remodeling."

Two days later, Nina sat in her grandmother's room waiting for the older woman to be wheeled back in after going for tests. She pretended to thumb through a women's magazine that her mother had brought a stack of, but she wasn't really interested in the articles on crocheting or easy, healthy meals.

Over the past couple of days, she'd practically moved in with her grandmother. She was thankful to Heidi, who had packed a bag for her and brought it to the hospital, making a trip back to Fantasy unnecessary. But the time clock on her return was quickly counting down. She'd have to go back sometime. She just didn't want it to be now. Not yet. Not yet.

"They have more attractive orthopedic shoes than that," her grandmother was saying to the nurse as she was wheeled back into the room. "I'll get you the name of a place that can take care of you. No need for a woman as attractive as you to pass up the opportunity to appeal to that young Dr. Monahan."

The nurse laughed. "I'm married with three kids, Mrs. Ross."

"Your point is? You never know what's going to happen tomorrow. A woman should always leave her options open."

The nurse laughed again and Nina got up to help transfer her grandmother back to the bed.

"Oh, for God's sake, I can get back into bed myself," Gladys protested. "Lord knows I've had enough practice."

Nina nearly choked on her own saliva, but the nurse appeared to have missed the sexual reference. Thank God for small favors.

"Still terrorizing the staff, I see," Nina said,

sitting back down in the chair and claiming the magazine again after the nurse had left.

"It's the only action to be found around here. Last night I tried to pick up the old guy in the room next door."

"What happened?"

"His wife called for a nurse to wheel me out."

Nina stared at her. "You hit on a guy in front of his wife?"

Gladys shrugged as she adjusted her blankets. "How was I supposed to know she'd just gone to the cafeteria for a cup of coffee? He never said anything. Obviously, he was leaving *his* options open."

She winked at Nina knowingly.

Nina had spent last night at her parents', deciding that it would be a good idea for her to get there early enough to have dinner with them considering she was accepting their hospitality.

"You're incorrigible."

"No, I'm alive. And so long as I'm alive, I'm going to be kicking."

"God, sometimes you really…"

Gladys raised a brow at her.

Nina caught her lip between her teeth and bit down. She didn't know where that opening comment had come from. While her grand-mother might embarrass her on occasion, mostly she found the older woman amusing and a fresh change from her ordinary, boring life.

Perhaps it was because her life wasn't so boring. Not anymore. And maybe it was because a part of her, just a tiny little part, blamed Gladys for putting thoughts into her head. If it weren't for those thoughts, she might never have gone ahead with Gauge's stupid plan. Might never have welcomed Kevin into her bed and then mistaken him for Gauge and slept with him, as well.

But that wasn't fair, was it? She was an adult woman more than capable of making her own decisions.

And, it was baldly apparent, of making her own mistakes.

"What were you going to say, child?" Gladys asked when she didn't continue.

Nina closed the magazine with a clap. "Can't you take anything seriously for two seconds?" She dropped the periodical on the pile of others her grandmother hadn't touched. "I mean, for God's sake, you just had a heart attack. Certainly that, more than anything, should give you a little food for thought."

"Thought about what, dear?"

Gladys reached for her makeup case on the side table and took her lipstick out, freshening up the color.

It was all Nina could do not to snatch it from her hand and toss the tube into the garbage can.

"Oh, I don't know. Maybe think twice about the way you're leading your life?"

"Like a warning bell from God to start living a less sinful life?"

Nina snapped her mouth closed, but managed to nod.

Lord, now she definitely sounded like her uptight mother.

"Yes," her grandmother said quietly. "Actually, this experience has made me stop to take stock of my life."

This surprised Nina.

"For about all of two seconds."

Nina gave an eye roll that almost hurt with its intensity.

"Now, don't you be doing that to me, missy. I'm still your grandmother, you know. And you'll show me respect."

"Then start acting like a grandmother."

Nina cringed at the words. How many times

growing up had she heard her mother say the same thing to Gladys? "When you start acting like a mother, I'll start treating you like mine," was a favorite.

"I'm sorry," she said quietly, averting her gaze. "That was uncalled for."

Gladys rearranged her blankets, trying to appear nonchalant even though Nina could see the words had bothered her. "Now I'm really curious about what happened."

Nina met her gaze head-on.

"So are you going to tell me what's going on? Or am I going to have to torture it out of you?"

15

"I'M LEAVING."

Kevin heard the words but it took a moment for them to register. It was nearly closing time and out of the corner of his eye, he'd watched Gauge approach the counter, as he had been doing at least three to four times a day since that fateful night. And he had every intention of ignoring him, as he had on those occasions.

But this time he looked up into his friend's eyes.

Gauge shrugged and glanced at their final customer browsing through the Clive Cussler selections. "I just thought I should tell you that I've decided it'll be best for everyone involved if I just packed up my things and moved on."

Kevin had imagined a lot of things over the past few days, but this certainly hadn't been one of them. He'd never have suspected such thoughts were going through Gauge's mind.

He'd thought he enjoyed his job and his one-third ownership of the store.

He didn't know what to say.

A part of him was glad for Gauge's words.

Another part wanted to tell him not to be so hasty.

Gauge ran his hand through his hair, tousling it even further. "I heard that Nina's coming back tonight and will be in the store tomorrow. So I think now's a good time."

Kevin smacked the last book from a new shipment he was scanning into the system on top of the stack. "You know, you do a goddamn lot of that. Coming up with ideas and making decisions you think are best for everybody else."

Gauge crossed his arms. "Tell me you don't want to see me leave."

Kevin clenched his jaw. "Right this minute? I'd like nothing better than to see your cheating ass disappear from this shop and my life."

He caught Gauge's cringe, but felt nothing more than satisfied at the reaction.

He moved the stack of books to the back counter where he could shelve them in the morning.

"Don't you think you at least owe her a goodbye?" he asked in a low, steady voice.

"Who? Nina?"

Kevin's jaw further clenched.

"No. I think she'd pretty much figured out what went down. And I'm probably the last person she wants to see."

"There you go. Speaking for other people again."

Kevin collapsed the shipping box and slid it under the counter before turning to face the other man.

"You know why I think you're leaving, Gauge?"

Gauge smirked. "No, Kevin, I don't. But I think you're about to tell me."

"You're damn right I'm going to tell you. You're leaving not out of some misplaced sense of duty, or because you're doing what you think is right. You're leaving because you're a goddamn coward."

That knocked the expression right off his face more effectively than if Kevin had hit him with his clenched fist.

"That's right. You're leaving because you can't face the music that you, yourself, created. Instead, you're running. Running away from this problem just like you've run away from all the other problems you've encountered in your life."

Neither of them said anything for a long moment. They merely stood, staring each other down.

"Are you saying you want me to stay?"

"I'm saying that you should at least stay to see what Nina has to say about all this."

"Have you spoken to her?"

Kevin straightened the flyers on the counter.

"Look who's calling who a coward."

Gauge turned to walk away. Kevin came out from behind the counter and grabbed his arm, forcing him to face him.

"Just what in the hell did you mean by that?"

"You seem to be the expert on human behavior lately, Kevin. You tell me."

Kevin forced himself to release his friend's arm, but it took all of his concentration not to give in to the desire to hit him again. "You know, you have a very bad habit of making assumptions."

"Maybe," Gauge admitted. "So tell me then why you haven't called her."

Kevin didn't have an answer for that.

"I know. It's because you think she might want me over you."

Kevin was going to hit him.

Gauge must have seen his intention in his eyes because backed out of slugging range.

"What happened the other night was a mistake, Kevin. Pure and simple. I said something that must have made her think I was the one who had spent the night with her and she acted on it. That's it. Nothing more, nothing less."

Kevin snorted. "You must have said something. Tell me, Gauge. Did you purposely say something that made her think that?"

"What?"

"You heard me. Did you purposely make her think that you were the one so you could have a run at that ass yourself?"

This time it looked as if Gauge might hit Kevin.

That surprised Kevin, and he took a small step back.

"You must not have a very high opinion of me."

"This minute? No, I don't."

"Did you ever stop to think for a moment that she might believe you incapable of sneaking into her bedroom late at night and doing all sorts of decadent things to her, Kevin? Fine, upstanding man that you are, from a good family. A good boy to the end, did you ever once consider that she might have thought you incapable of having anonymous sex with her?"

Kevin froze.

"No. I didn't think so."

He turned to go again and this time Kevin let him.

Gauge stopped just this side of the stockroom door and dropped his head before shifting slightly to give Kevin a sidelong glance.

"Grow up, Kevin."

Kevin blinked at him.

"It's time you understood that there's a big difference between sex and love."

"Of course, you would be the expert on both."

Gauge didn't say anything for a long moment, and then he rubbed his chin. "No, I'm not. But I do think I have a hell of a lot more experience in this than you do. Including in the love department." He looked in the other direction briefly before looking back. "What Nina and I did the other night…that was just sex."

"And what she and I did?"

"That was the love that made her go looking for that sex."

Kevin wasn't sure he understood what, exactly, that meant. But he remained where he was, watching as Gauge picked up the guitar and bag he had waiting at the door and then walked through it without saying another word.

NINA PURPOSELY waited until after midnight to pull in to the parking lot of the store. She held her breath as she looked around, not seeing any other cars, and then let the air out in a quiet whoosh.

She hadn't known what to expect. Or even what she'd been hoping to find. But seeing that everything was normal on a regular Thursday night reassured her somehow.

Yet she still felt outside herself.

When the winter chill began to invade the warm interior of the car, she climbed out, grabbing her bag from the back and then headed toward the outside stairs leading to her apartment. Someone had shoveled and salted the wooden slats. Likely Heidi, who she had asked to look after Ernie while she was away. She trudged up the steps much as she had every day over the past four years.

Then again, it was nothing like it, was it? Because she was no longer the same person she had been during that time. Within a week's span, she had evolved into someone else. Exactly who that person was, she didn't know. But she understood that she would never be that other woman again. The one who haphazardly picked her dates and stuck with them for a long period before discovering they weren't for her.

So, in that regard, she supposed Gauge's plan had worked.

Unfortunately, the lesson had come with a high price.

She let herself into her apartment, closing the door behind her and dropping her bag to the floor. She bent to take off her boots, a task made doubly difficult by an effusive Ernie. Nina patted him, always finding it strange that twenty pounds of cat flesh could nearly knock her over.

"Did you miss me, boy?" She finally stepped out of the boots and into her waiting fuzzy slippers and then picked the purring feline up, holding him out in front of her.

"I missed you, too, baby. I missed you, too."

She cuddled him close to her chest and kissed the side of his neck even as she walked farther into the apartment, switching on lights as she went.

She wasn't sure what she'd expected. Perhaps that since she had changed so much internally, her external surroundings would some-how have also been altered. But, aside from the small pile of mail on the hall table, a fresh carton of milk in the refrigerator and a note from Heidi lying on top of a covered plate of pastry, nothing had changed.

She picked up the note and read aloud, "Welcome home."

Home.

She put the note back down and then took the milk and a bowl out, giving Ernie a rare treat because too much gave him diarrhea.

Ernie leaped down from her arms, purring up a storm as he lapped both the milk and her pats up.

She wandered through the rest of the rooms, switching on the television in her bedroom while she stripped out of her clothes. Conan O'Brien was interviewing someone she didn't recognize as she moved into the connecting bathroom and climbed into the shower. She waited until the water got to temperature and then stood under the pounding jets.

And just like that, everything she'd been able to avoid for the past few days collapsed on top of her because she was no longer able to keep it aloft.

What had she done?

Worry over her grandmother had kept her from succumbing to the sadness that pressed in on her from all sides. But now that Gladys was going home from the hospital tomorrow, and was well on the way to recovery, she no longer had that excuse to keep her from facing what had happened.

She remembered the hurt expression on Kevin's face when he'd caught her and Gauge. But it wasn't really Gauge, was it? Oh, physically it may have been, but she'd thought he was her mystery lover. So, with or without the blindfold, that was the man she'd been seeking out.

Only Kevin had been that man.

She knew that now. As plainly as she knew what day it was.

And she also knew that with one impulsive act, she'd ruined everything that had taken them three years to build.

The store.

Their friendship.

Her hot tears battled the shower spray as she cried.

How could she have been so stupid? How could she have missed all the signals?

Long minutes later, the hot water began to turn cold. She lethargically shut it off and then reached for a towel, Ernie giving himself a tongue bath on the mat at her feet.

She stepped over him and went straight to her bed, not even bothering with a nightgown or panties as she wrapped her hair in the towel and then climbed under the covers. The canned laughter coming from the television sounded strange to her so she shut it off and lay in the dark for long moments.

Waiting. She seemed to be waiting for something. For the emotions crowding her chest to dissipate. For someone, anyone to do something that would alleviate her own pain. Take it away. Tell her that it was okay, she'd made a mistake, and that everything would go back to being normal in the morning.

Only she knew no one could do that. Because it wouldn't be okay. Everything had changed.

And nothing would ever be the same again.

16

THE NEXT DAY passed in a blur. As did the day after that.

Nina kept her attention on the café and everything that had happened in her absence. It had taken her half a day before she realized that the music center counter had essentially been closed. Heidi had caught her staring in that direction and said, "Yeah, surprising, Gauge's leaving like that and everything."

Gauge had left? What did she mean that Gauge had left?

Of course, there was one person who could answer that question for her. But Kevin refused to meet her gaze whenever they crossed paths. And the cold vibes he gave off made her shiver. So she hadn't dared ask for fear of what he might say. Or of how he might interpret her curiosity.

Stupid, stupid, stupid.

She decided that at day's end she would stop being stupid and just come out and ask him. Let him think what he wanted. Personal mess aside, they were still business partners. And this concerned a one-third interest in their business.

Nina walked into the bookstore, surprised by the large group of cheering children. She'd forgotten that it was Saturday and story time. The latest Salamander book was out today and it seemed everyone under the age of ten was ecstatic. She stopped at the center's counter, pretending to go over notes on a clipboard when she was really curious about what was going on in the public gathering area.

Since her return from Detroit, she'd made a point of avoiding the spot. She hadn't wanted to be reminded of the incident that had started out as a harmless erotic encounter and had turned all of their lives upside down. She was surprised to find that the leather couch and chairs had been removed, replaced by a series of uncomfortable-looking, multicolored plastic chairs, with a column of stackable siblings nearby.

She frowned. What had happened to the furniture?

"All right, everyone!" Kevin's assistant called out to the rambunctious children. "Last one to sit in a neat row is a spoilsport."

Nina smiled slightly as the children all hurried to get into position. No one, of course, was labeled anything. It was a mere means to an end, and John had already taken the chair in front of them, the brand-new edition in the Salamander series in his hands.

That was odd....

Nina looked around. Kevin was usually the reader. He loved the kids. And the kids loved him in return. She could count on two fingers the times he hadn't handled Saturday afternoon story time. When he'd been sick with the flu and hadn't wanted to pass around the germs, and when his mother had died.

With everything well in control, she picked up the clipboard and headed into the main bookstore section, her gaze seeking Kevin.

There he was. Shelving copies of J. D. Robb's latest in the mainstream section.

"Is something wrong?" she asked his back.

She noticed the way his shoulders stiffened, as if she had just pelted him with ice balls rather than words.

"Excuse me?" He finished shelving the books in his hands and turned toward her.

"Are you sick?"

His eyes narrowed.

She sighed and gestured toward the children. "You love reading to the kids."

"I'm fine."

He turned back toward his task.

Nina stood staring at him for a long moment. This avoidance stuff was getting old, but quick.

Of course, her using story time as an excuse to talk to him was little more than avoidance at its best. But, damn it, she didn't know what else to do.

She began to turn away, and then recalled that there was one item that they could discuss now that was directly related to what was going on. She gathered her wits about her and decided that now was as good a time as any.

"Heidi told me Gauge left."

She thought it impossible that Kevin's shoulders could stiffen any further. She was proven wrong.

"Could you please expound on the meaning of *left?*"

He didn't respond.

She grasped his arm. "Damn it, Kevin, talk to me."

He turned cold eyes on her and she shivered.

"Does *left* mean that he's gone on an extended vacation somewhere? Or does *left* mean that he's moved on...permanently?"

Finally, Kevin faced her fully. "Why? Do you want to pick up where you left off?"

Nina's palm itched with the desire to slap him where he stood.

"That's too bad. Because he's left. For good. No forwarding address, no plans to return. Gone."

Nina's heart gave a squeeze. She'd hit rock bottom, convinced things couldn't possibly get any worse. And while she'd feared that Gauge had left town, hearing Kevin say the words made her feel sick to her stomach.

"Why didn't you tell me?" she whispered, curious about the flicker of sadness on his face.

"I figured he would have told you."

He was lying. She could tell because Kevin had never been any good at falsehoods. Even white lies probably made him break out in hives. It wasn't the way he was made.

"No," she said quietly. "That's not what I'm talking about."

She searched his face for some sign that what had passed between them on that one magical night remained. She found nothing.

"I'm not talking about Gauge, Kevin. I'm talking about what happened between us."

MUCH LATER that day, after having closed the store at six, Kevin lifted a sledgehammer, aiming it for the half wall that separated the dining room from the kitchen of his house. His muscles bunched underneath his T-shirt, his teeth were clenched, and he experienced a brief moment of satisfaction as the hammer met with hard plaster, knocking a hole the size of a plate in the wall. A hole that mirrored the one in his chest.

Damn, damn, damn.

He recalled Nina's face earlier when she'd asked him about Gauge. Remembered his own visceral response to her inquiry. The way the jealousy that had been festering in him since the night he'd caught them together had boiled over, scalding her with its acidity.

He swung again, the crash momentarily eclipsing the thud-thud of his heart.

Over the past few days he'd emptied the house of almost all traces of his parents, choosing only a few items that he might like to pass on to his children, if he ever had any, and his mother's favorites. The rest he'd given to the Salvation Army and family members.

Which left him a clean canvas on which to work.

His mother had kept an old-fashioned house. The type where doilies were draped over decades-old furniture, the paint colors and wallpaper muted and very feminine.

It was nothing like him.

He wasn't entirely clear on what drove him now. He merely knew a strong desire to begin taking control over his life rather than passively allowing things to happen around him.

Hell, his mother had been dead for two years and he still watered her plants as if she would be returning any minute.

The plants were among the first things to go. A neighbor had been quick to take them off his hands, along with a good number of pieces of overly ornate furniture. Which was fine with him. Good riddance was all he could say.

He finished demolishing the half wall and stood staring at the large pile of debris while he wiped the sweat from his brow with his shoulder.

As things stood, the entire house was in various stages of renovation. He'd even finally taken over the master bedroom, ordering in new furniture, although he hadn't been completely able to get rid of his old. His boyhood room still sat much the same as it had been when he was growing up, the only exception being the double bed he'd gotten when he was a senior in high school.

He allowed the sledgehammer to drop from his grip and braced it against another wall, and then he stepped over the debris to get a beer from the refrigerator. He popped open the top and took a deep pull while walking through the first floor, taking in all the work he'd done and all that had yet to be done.

Late last night he'd realized he'd accomplished the first part of his intention: he no longer recognized the place as his parents'. Bare walls, carpet pulled up, old doors taken down to the basement to be painted, the house could have been a new one he'd recently moved into. One in need of lots of TLC.

Not unlike himself, he realized.

An image of Nina popped into his mind and he immediately ousted it. She had no place in his plans.

But what were those plans, beyond reclaiming his parents' house as his own?

He couldn't say. But he knew that whatever they were, they would evolve naturally as a result of his activities.

The rap of someone knocking on his front door made him frown. Had the neighbors called the sheriff on him again? He wasn't wearing a watch, so he couldn't be sure of the time, but he was positive it wasn't that late.

He swung open the door then stood staring at the last person he expected to find standing on his porch.

Nina.

It was a cold February night, but somehow looking into Kevin's eyes as the expression in them changed from open curiosity to indifference made it feel even colder.

Nina snuggled farther into her white down jacket and then looked over her shoulder at the quiet night.

"Mind if I come in?" she asked when he hadn't said anything, hadn't even acknowledged her appearance beyond staring at her as if he wanted her gone from his porch.

He opened the door wider and then stood leaning against it, leaving her a narrow path that required she come in physical contact with him when she passed.

Nina caught her breath at the rock-hard feel of his abs as she brushed against them, the scent of sawdust and beer filling her nose.

She blinked at the scene before her as Kevin closed the door. While the place looked exactly the same on the outside, inside…well, she wouldn't have known she was in the right place had she not just come in via the familiar front door…or if Kevin weren't standing in the middle of the room, his arms crossed, a half-empty beer bottle dangling from the fingers of his right hand.

Nina swallowed hard, incapable of holding his penetrating gaze as she stepped around the living room, peering into the dining area and then the kitchen. "Did you do all this yourself?"

She was guessing that he had, if the dusty old T-shirt and jeans he wore were any indication. Her gaze flicked to his rock-solid form and she swallowed hard again.

Why hadn't she noticed how buff he was before? Yes, he may have done a good job disguising his physique under oversized denim shirts and loose jeans, but still…

She caught herself staring at his bulging biceps, probably made larger by the physical work he was doing around the house. But that couldn't take all the credit. She already knew he was hands-on when it came to his coaching hockey and soccer.

She guessed that maybe she just hadn't looked closely enough. Had never had much reason to.

Until now.

She cleared her throat. "Look, Kevin, I…"

She what?

Suddenly, coming over here didn't seem a good idea. She'd been at home sharing a quiet meal with Ernie when she'd decided to have it out with Kevin once and for all. He needed to understand that she hadn't intended what had happened. She needed to make her point of view clear.

She needed to tell him she was sorry.

She glanced into his stony face. Unfortunately, he wasn't making any of it easier.

17

DAMN IT ALL to hell. Kevin wanted to hate the woman in front of him. Wanted, at the very least, to hold on to his anger. But as he took in her beautiful face, and watched the way her emotions played out across her features, the way she unconsciously stuffed her hands deeper into the pockets of her short jacket, he felt a growing desire to kiss her.

Equal only to his longing to punish her.

He took another long pull from his beer, perfectly aware that he hadn't offered her anything and that she looked awkward, as if feeling unwelcome.

And she was unwelcome. He didn't want her there. Didn't want her anywhere near him where she could wreak more havoc over his once neatly aligned life.

He finished the beer and then placed the empty bottle on the stairs. He wasn't aware he'd stepped closer to Nina until she backed away from him, an expression of surprise on her face.

"Why did you come here, Nina?" he asked, his gaze flicking over her chin and mouth and then boring into her eyes. "What do you want?"

His voice was low and gravelly as he backed her against the wall and then braced his hand against it beside her head, blocking a direct route to the door.

"I...I..."

He watched her mouth work its way around a response that didn't appear imminent.

Instead, she licked her lips.

The simple, provocative action made Kevin's awareness level leap.

He leaned his head close enough to kiss her, his gaze on her mouth.

"Haven't you done enough damage already?" he asked quietly. "Did you come over here to do more?"

Pain shot through her beautiful blue eyes. Pain that he didn't want to see, was in no mindset to acknowledge, much less accept.

"I came over here to tell you I was sorry," she finally whispered, searching his face.

She was sorry.

Yeah, well, so was he.

That and a dollar might get them a loaf of bread on sale.

Kevin braced his other hand against the wall, effectively trapping her.

"Uh-uh. I don't think that's why you came here tonight."

She swallowed hard, her pupils briefly widening, but whether it was in fear or awareness, he couldn't be sure.

And he didn't care.

Damn it, he'd spent the days since their night together in a ceaseless state of agitation. Of having had a taste of something wonderful and then being denied anything more.

His heartbeat sped up as he breathed in her sweet scent, brushing his nose against her jawline and up over her cheek and temple.

"I think you came here for this."

He kissed her.

NINA'S PULSE leaped as she watched Kevin lean in toward her. She anticipated his kiss…except it wasn't as she remembered. Where his kisses had been exploratory and passionate before, now they were rough and punishing.

She moaned in pain and in longing, kissing him back even though a small voice told her that she should be pushing him away. But she was so relieved that he was showing her some attention that she couldn't help but respond. Her hands found the front of his shirt, ready to push against him. Instead they melded against the hard wall of his chest. She felt his heartbeat against her palm, finding some comfort that he was as worked up as she was, feeling connected to him by more than just their kiss.

He plundered the depths of her mouth, bruising her lips. Nina sighed against him, hot tears welling behind her closed eyelids.

She'd been so afraid that this part of their relationship was over—that they might not even be able to find their way back to anything, let alone friendship—that the relief that suffused her muscles was almost overwhelming.

Kevin moved his right hand from the wall and grasped her breast through the thick jacket. Frustrated by the clothing, he yanked the zipper down and pulled the coat over her shoulder before clamping his hand back over the hypersensitive flesh through her shirt. Nina shivered at his branding touch, shrugging to rid herself of the garment completely and letting it fall to the floor.

Kevin moved in closer, pressing his hard length against her stomach before shoving his knee between hers and lifting her until only he and the wall held her upright. She grasped his shoulders and moaned, his leg pushing into her womanhood with insistent urgency. She curved her hands under his arms and gripped his shoulders from behind, needing him closer yet, wanting him to claim her in whatever manner he desired even as she tried to reconcile the unrelenting man making love to her now to the gentle, passionate man from before.

He tugged on her hair from the back and she dropped her head, giving him access to her neck. His stubble burned her skin as he kissed her fervently, seeming to need to hurt her and love her equally.

Nina slid her hands from his shoulders, following his spine down to the waist of his jeans where she wasted no time pulling his T-shirt out and tunneling her fingers underneath, dragging them against his warm skin even as he reclaimed her mouth.

The leg between hers disappeared, as did his mouth. Nina blinked open her eyes to find him standing a couple of feet away from her, breathing deeply and staring darkly at her from under his tousled hair. He resembled a wild animal on the first day of spring, and she felt like a mating female trapped by his gaze.

Nina flattened her palms against the wall behind her, fighting to catch her own breath, to gather her wits about her.

Was that it? Was he going to ask her to leave? Tell her never to come back?

She saw that he wanted to. Wanted to ban her from his life.

She also saw that he wanted her to stay.

"Damn it, Nina," he ground out between clenched teeth. "I don't want to want you. Not anymore."

She blinked, unclear as to his meaning.

Did that mean that he had always wanted her?

She didn't dare ask for fear that she would nudge him in a direction she didn't want him to go.

His gaze raked her from head to toe and then slowly back up again. Nina felt as if she were on the auction block and it was too late to make herself more attractive to her buyer. She could only stand there and allow him to look his fill, come to whatever conclusion he would.

"Don't," he said.

She hadn't realized she'd taken a step forward until he held up his hand to ward her off.

"I'm sorry," she said, so softly she nearly didn't hear her own words. "I'm so sorry, Kevin. I…"

His eyes narrowed to sharp slits.

"I don't know what I can possibly say to make any of this better. But I know I need to try."

"For the business?"

"For us."

"There is no us." His expression was fierce, accusing.

"But wasn't that the entire point of this whole stupid plan?" she asked. "That I wouldn't know which one of you I spent the night with? So I wouldn't confuse sex with intimacy?"

"I never should have done it."

"But you did."

He nodded. "Yes, I did. And now you've slept with both of us."

"I never intended for that to be the case."

"Didn't you?"

"Of course not!"

He was like a statue fixed to a specific spot on the floor while she moved ever forward toward him.

"Is that what you think?" she whispered.

He didn't blink. Then he ran his hand over his face as if trying to wake himself from a bad dream. "I don't know what to think anymore."

Nina forced her gaze away from him to the staircase beyond. She felt like the gutted house around her, her exterior layers stripped away, leaving her raw and vulnerable.

Then again, he had been renovating a house that didn't need to be changed.

She squinted at Kevin, wondering if she was still thinking about a house.

"Ironic, isn't it?" she said quietly. "We agreed to this so I wouldn't confuse sex with a relationship." She tilted her head, making sure she had his attention. "But now it's you who's doing that."

His anger seemed to return tenfold and he moved the two steps required to bring him to stand directly in front of her. "What?"

Nina shrugged, trying for nonchalance. Instead, she quaked inside, every inch of her aware of his nearness, of the conflict that raged inside of him. "I thought I was making love to you," she finally whispered.

He grasped her arm roughly. "You didn't know who was in your bedroom that night."

Nina winced. While she knew he would never really hurt her, there were other ways to inflict pain. "I didn't. Not until it was too late. Which essentially means that I had sex with you both times."

"You screwed Gauge."

She shook her head. "No, Kevin, I didn't. Physically, yes. But psychologically I was with the man I had invited into my bed so many nights before." She swallowed thickly. "I was making love with you."

He grabbed her other arm and brought her flush up against him. Nina straightened her shoulders, staring him down, challenging him to deny what she was saying was true.

Instead he kissed her.

KEVIN TRIED to keep his anger in check. Tried to keep his fingers from denting the soft flesh of Nina's arms. But he couldn't help himself. A maelstrom of emotion swirled within him at her quietly spoken words.

Was it true what she was saying? That, after all was said and done, he was confusing sex for a relationship? That what she had shared with Gauge had been nothing but sex? And only because she had thought it was him?

He crushed his mouth down over hers, wanting so badly to believe her. To find truth in her words so that he might begin the long journey toward healing himself.

Toward healing them both.

But the fury inside him refused to budge. It was searching for an outlet that he had found temporarily in house renovations. But that wasn't enough. He wanted…needed to demand his pound of flesh from the woman responsible for the resentment, the pain.

He held her still as he plundered her mouth. She tasted good. Too good.

A part of him had believed their one night together would assuage the desire he'd always harbored for her. Instead, it had only increased it. He wanted her more than he'd ever wanted her before.

Which was, he reasoned, the cause for his visceral reaction to seeing her with another man.

Nina tried to raise her hands to his hips. He instantly released his grip on her arms and crowded her to his chest, holding her tight. He briefly closed his eyes, breathing in the sweet scent of her hair, absorbing the warmth from her soft body.

His own body roared in response.

He stepped forward until her back met with the wall again and reclaimed his hold on her breast, kneading the mound of flesh, feeling the tightness of her nipple through her shirt. He roughly stripped the white cotton from her, following up with her bra, until she stood topless in front of him. Her breath came in shallow gasps, causing her breasts to heave. He grasped both of them in his hands and lowered his head to take the peak of first one, then the other, into his mouth, laving them, sucking on them hungrily.

He'd waited so very long to taste her fragrant flesh. Three years and two months, to be exact. He'd ached with want for her, yearned to wedge himself between her thighs. And for one, sweet night, he'd finally gotten to do it all.

And then he'd allowed fear to take over. Fear that if he told her it was him, she would attach herself to him just like she had attached herself to the other transient men in her life. Fear that he would fall deeper and deeper in love with her, only to be kicked to the curb after six months just like the others.

He hadn't realized how much of a role fear had played in his life until now. As an only child, he'd been raised to be fearful of everything.

Throughout grade school he'd been afraid that if he read aloud, everyone would figure out it took him longer to make out the words than it did the other kids, the diagnosis of dyslexia still to come. In high school, he'd been afraid of hooking up with the wrong girl, of facing his parents' disapproval, parents who had doted on him, perhaps a little too much, looking at every aspect of his life under a magnifying glass simply because beyond the house he was in they didn't have much else to consider.

He'd been terrified that if he didn't choose the right woman he'd be made a fool of. Or, worse, hurt the way he was hurting now.

He switched his attention back up to her mouth, kissing her and then kissing her again, as if seeking to transfer the pain he was experiencing to her. Make her take it because it wasn't what he wanted.

He reached for the fastener to her jeans and yanked it open, only semi aware of her gasp as she gripped his shoulders. Her reaction emboldened him somehow, rather than deterring him. In small, impatient movements, he pulled off her shoes and socks, her pants and her panties until she stood naked and trembling in front of him.

He pulled back to take in his fill of her.

He'd always known she would be beautiful. High, full breasts, narrow waist, lush hips and soft thighs. What he hadn't bargained for was the mole near her navel. The small scar on her shoulder, probably from a childhood mishap. Things that made her uniquely Nina.

And all combined to make him want to claim her entirely, completely as his.

18

KEVIN MOVED his hand down Nina's belly, feeling the trembling there, then moved on to the cleanly shaven area that lay between her thighs. He heard her quick intake of breath as his fingers probed the engorged flesh, pinching her enlarged bud and then sliding inward between the slick folds. So wet....

He thrust two fingers up inside her and she cried out. Her surprised response fed his need to possess her. He withdrew the fingers and then thrust again, taking in the rocking of her breasts as she clutched the wall behind her for balance. He caught one of the stiff peaks in his mouth, running his tongue along the nipple and then sucking deeply as he thrust again.

She moaned, her juices covering his fingers, lubricating his movements, and he felt her muscles contract as she reached orgasm.

The knowledge that she'd climaxed both pleased and angered him. He looked down, shocked to find he was still dressed. After pulling a condom out of his wallet, he quickly stripped off his clothes until he stood nude before her. He watched her eyes follow his movements, the color in her cheeks high, her pink lips swollen and bruised from his attentions.

He didn't waste time with foreplay. Didn't have the patience to make sure she was ready for him. He sheathed his rock-hard erection and then roughly grasped her right leg, hooking it over his hip as he positioned his shaft against her, and then he thrust into her to the hilt.

A low, rolling moan filled his ear as Nina clutched him, her head next to his. He grasped her hips, tilting them slightly forward as he thrust again, insistently, angrily, seeking something he couldn't name, refused to define. He thrust again, and again, forcing her up the wall each time he did. His blood surged through him like dark acid, propelling him, drawing his muscles taut, filling him with a brutal desire to show her he wasn't a man to be toyed with, used, betrayed and then tossed by the wayside.

Long before he'd planned, or expected, he felt

his climax build in the pit of his stomach, drawing more and more energy and then exploding in one burst of dark, hot light.

Kevin became slowly aware of two things at once as he fought to catch his breath. One, that Nina had collapsed against him like a rag doll.

Two, that she was crying.

NINA FELT as though Kevin had created a tunnel straight up to her heart and then ripped that vital organ out, leaving her love to bleed from the open wound.

She couldn't move and was having a hard time breathing as she fought for control over her shredded emotions. But there was no control to be had. Kevin's cold, hard lovemaking had left her a willing victim to his selfish desires, yet an equal participant as a shadowy side of herself responded to his rough attentions, as if perhaps believing she was deserving of his punishment.

"Jesus," she heard him grind out.

She found the energy to clutch him, not wanting him to leave her hanging there. If he pulled away from her, surely she would bleed to death.

Instead he grasped her head in his hands, tipping her face to look up into his.

The relief she felt at the concern on his face was more than she could bear, and a sob ripped from her throat.

"Did I hurt you?" he asked, kissing her eyelids one by one, then resting his mouth against her forehead. "Oh, God, did I hurt you?"

Nina found a way to shake her head slightly. "No…not physically.…"

They stood there for long minutes, neither of them saying anything, as Nina slowly felt the wild torrent of pain within her begin to subside. She knew a chill, but this time the draughty house had caused it.

Before she had an opportunity to prepare herself for the move, Kevin swept her up into his arms, tucking her head into his neck as he strode toward the stairs.

Despite his previous behavior, she couldn't help but cling to him, praying that whatever had gone on inside him had lessened. She didn't think she could handle anything else.

She was concentrating so hard on the line of his jaw and his set expression that she hadn't realized he'd taken her up to what she assumed was his bedroom until he laid her gently down on top of a king-size bed. It was dark up here and he didn't turn on a lamp. Instead she watched as he disposed of the used condom. She scooted farther up on the mattress until she reached the pillows. He helped her pull down the jacquard comforter and then climbed into bed with her, cradling her close to his chest.

Nina felt like crying anew at this change in him.

"I must have hurt you more than I knew," she whispered, stroking her fingertips over the light hair that sprinkled his chest.

His embrace tightened. "That's no reason to do what I just did," he said into her hair, his chin resting on the top of her head. "I'm sorry, Nina. I'm so sorry if I caused you any pain."

Her throat grew tight. "Seems like we just keep hurting each other."

He didn't say anything for a long moment. Minutes passed and she began to think he'd fallen asleep, except that she hadn't detected any change in his breathing.

"You know, I understand now that I lived so much of my life in fear that I never invested myself emotionally in any relationship outside the one I had with my parents."

Nina stared sightlessly at the opposite wall as she listened to his softly spoken words.

"While I've dated, I did it more out of satisfying first my adolescent hormonal needs, and then when I was older, for sexual release. But I never loved any of them. Never allowed myself to."

She shifted slightly so that she could look into his shadowed face. The light from downstairs made its way up into the hallway and a dim swath cut a path across the bed.

"Why?" she asked.

He shook his head slightly. "I don't.know. Maybe it was because my parents were so much older. They had reached the age where life had become so precious to them that they unknowingly passed on that same caution on to me. Or perhaps because of our love for books, we learned the lessons taught there, so we didn't learn them through living. I don't know." He tucked his chin into his chest and looked at her. She caught her breath at the seriousness of his expression. "What I am coming to understand is that while chronologically I'm thirty-one, psychologically I'm afraid I've been acting like an adolescent who just got dumped by my first love."

Nina's heart skipped a beat.

She'd recognized earlier her own expanding feelings for him. Knew instinctively to permit him to take whatever liberties he needed to move beyond his anger at her, at their situation. She'd progressed beyond simple attraction and desire. She'd always loved him as a friend; now she was coming to love him as a man.

"I do love you, you know," he spoke the words quietly. "I probably have since the first moment I laid eyes on you."

She closed her eyes and smiled softly, remembering the moment. He'd been awkward and hesitant. She'd been flattered.

And then they'd both met Gauge and she'd forced any romantic thoughts of Kevin aside in exchange for friendship between the three of them.

"Gauge knew that," Kevin said, surprising her. Not with what he said, but that he'd mentioned Gauge in a way that didn't include anger. "He knew I was in love with you and practically forced me to go into your apartment that night."

Nina rubbed her foot against his leg, feeling his rough hair against her sensitive skin. "You didn't want to come?"

"That was the problem. I wanted it too much."

He shifted so that they were lying side by side, his gaze capturing hers in the semidarkness.

"I've wanted you so badly for so long that I

ached with it. I'd watch you from across the store
and feel such a longing that I didn't recognize
life without that same longing. It wasn't just
physical." He kissed her, caressing her arm with
long, gentle strokes. He smiled. "Oh, there was
definitely that, but somehow it evolved into
something much, much more over the years. I
wanted to protect you. I wanted to watch you
grow old. I wanted to be the source for your
smiles, your laughter."

Nina looked down. While she could attest
to her current blossoming love for him, she
couldn't say she'd felt the same way he did. She
supposed that part of that might be because there
was only one of her and two of them.

Would Kevin feel the same way now had there
been another female in the equation?

She blinked to look into his eyes again. Actually, she suspected that he would. Because she
believed him, saw the truth in his words. And
was able to go back and connect the dots. She
could understand why he'd never dated anyone
for long, and shunned her attempts to set him up
with her friends.

It wasn't that he hadn't wanted them. It was
that he had wanted her.

"Then why not tell me then?" she asked. "Afterward…during. I don't care. Why didn't you tell me you were the one that night?"

Kevin's small smile made her heart leap. "Because I'd convinced myself that you would do the same to me that you'd done to the other men in your life. You'd fall instantly in love, and things would be great for six months, and then you'd get over me just like all the others."

Nina curved her arms around him and held him tightly, unable to imagine his fear. His hand softly stroked her back.

"I could have handled anything…but not that. Having you and then being forced to let you go."

Nina drew back, staring deeply into his eyes. The naked emotion there, the pure love, caused her heart to expand in her chest.

She'd known love. Or thought she had. But never had she been loved in the way Kevin was professing. The way she saw there in the depths of his eyes, warming the very edges of her heart.

She leaned in and kissed him. He kissed her back, the action tender and soft.

Instantly, she melted against him, falling back into the feathery down of sensation. A sensation that he effortlessly created merely by kissing her.

Only there was nothing truly effortless about it, was there? He'd gone through a hell she'd never be able to understand.

But by opening herself up to his love, she knew that she wouldn't be able to help herself from loving him back as fully as he loved her.

She rubbed the arch of her foot against the top of his, then she hooked her leg over his and lifted it until it lay over his hip. His semi-aroused penis pressed against her stomach. With a roll of his hips, it rested against her thigh, mere millimeters away from where she wanted it most.

Kevin deepened their kiss, as if unable to get enough of her. And she suddenly felt the same urgency, holding on to him tighter than she'd ever held on to anyone before.

He released her to reach toward the nightstand.

"No," she whispered. "I want…need to feel you…."

He didn't say anything for a long moment and didn't respond to her kissing him.

"Nina…."

She kissed either side of his mouth. "Hmm?"

"If you get pregnant…"

She held him tighter and kissed him head-on.

"If I get pregnant…I can't think of anyone's baby I'd love to have more."

She felt the tension leave his shoulders but he still wasn't kissing her back.

"A child is more than a six-month commitment."

She smiled against his mouth. "I know."

"Are you saying…"

"Shh," she said, rubbing her breasts against his chest and her womanhood against his now rock-hard arousal. "Let's pass that bridge when we come to it…."

He groaned and grabbed her hips, holding her still so he could thrust upward into her to the hilt.

Nina shuddered to the core at the feel of his unsheathed flesh claiming hers.

So, so nice….

He stroked her again…and then again…and she knew that she would do anything, whatever it took, to keep this man loving her.

19

A week later...

CLOSING TIME. And it couldn't have come a moment too soon.

Nina switched off the light to the kitchen, picked up her large cup of latte from the coffee counter, and then strode through the store, much as she'd done almost every night of the past three years.

The lights in the music center were already turned off by John, the assistant promoted to section manager. Still, Nina's steps slowed as she passed the main counter in the middle of the room.

A sound in the bookstore section caused her to look in the direction. She smiled and continued on to where she looked forward to seeing Kevin.

The past week...

She shivered, thinking it ironic that she was

surrounded by millions of words on the printed page and couldn't find the appropriate one to describe what had transpired over the past seven days.

More often than not, she'd slept at Kevin's house, although sleeping had played a very small role in what happened when she climbed willingly into his bed at night.

Magical....

Magnificent....

Exquisite....

All came near describing her time with Kevin, but still fell woefully short of painting the full picture.

She neared the counter to find Kevin bent over picking up what appeared to be books that had fallen.

"All out?" she asked, referring to any customers that might have been lingering inside the store.

"Just locked the door after the last one," he said over his shoulder.

Nina paused, considering the view of his perfect backside in snug jeans before smiling and moving on toward the fireplace. Balancing her mug carefully, she sank down into the new overstuffed couch and sighed, staring into the flames.

Minutes later, Kevin joined her, sitting next to her instead of across the way as he had once done.

She lifted her head from the back of the cushion to allow him to put his arm there and then leaned into him, leisurely kissing his neck before turning her attention back to her latte.

"What a day, huh?" she said quietly.

"You can say that again."

Today a highly topical book had become available and they'd been inundated with customers looking to buy it, turning it instantly into a red-hot bestseller. A good percentage of them hadn't even bothered waiting to get home before cracking it open, instead taking it with them into the café where they'd packed the tables, keeping both her and Kevin and the rest of the staff busy over the course of the day.

Nina's feet were killing her and the heels of her hands ached from spending so much of the day kneading and rolling out dough.

She took a long sip of her latte, her gaze drawn to the chair in front of the fireplace.

She went still.

Although usually the armchair was positioned next to the second chair across from her, someone had pulled it so that it was angled more directly in front of the fire…much as Gauge had used to do.

She could almost see him sitting on the edge of the cushion, his guitar parked on his knee as he strummed a few chords.

She felt his absence as surely as she felt the cold when she opened the front door.

She hadn't realized she'd sighed until Kevin tightened his grip around her, caressing her arm.

"I know. Seems strange not to have him here, doesn't it?"

Nina shifted her head to look up at his strong profile. As she had been, he was staring at the empty chair.

She had purposely gone out of her way not to bring Gauge up, instead stepping aside to allow Kevin to make any business decisions that needed attention, such as the promotion of John to section manager, the processing of the power of attorney Gauge had left in his wake, and a million other little details she guessed might be involved in a major part of the store being absent.

She wasn't sure why she still didn't feel comfortable bringing up Gauge around Kevin. Perhaps it was because their relationship was still so new and she didn't want to introduce a reminder that might imperil it.

She was thankful now that whatever journey Kevin had been making had brought him back to a level of comfort in speaking about Gauge.

She took another sip of latte, surprised she had almost finished it. "Do you think he'd be surprised to find we're now a couple?"

Kevin settled a little more comfortably into the cushions and stretched his feet to rest on the coffee table. "I don't think so."

She scooted her legs closer to his, reveling in the feel of him against her. "I don't think so, either."

That night seemed so long ago, even though Nina knew only a few short days had passed. It seemed so surreal in light of everything that had gone on since, that it was almost easy to think that it had been a dream.

Almost.

Sometimes Kevin might grasp her hips a little too tightly, thrust into her a little too hard, and she knew that he still felt a need to claim her in a way that no man ever had...Gauge included.

"I miss him," Kevin said.

She smiled. "Yeah, me, too."

She lifted her cup, thinking it was about time

they called it a day. Tonight they were staying at her place, Ernie having made such a fuss this morning when she returned from Kevin's that she didn't have the heart to leave him alone again.

She took the last sip of her latte…and choked on something that had been in the cup.

She jackknifed upright, coughing until her eyes watered.

"Aw, hell," Kevin said, patting her lightly on the back.

She gestured with her hands, indicating he should hit her harder.

He gave her a good whack and the object flew out of her mouth and into her waiting hands.

Nina's eyes went wide as she stared at the object she held. She used the left sleeve of her shirt to wipe at the dampness on her cheeks and then turned toward Kevin.

He grinned at her. "Not exactly the way I saw this going down." He scratched his chin. "Don't you ever look into your cup before you drink?"

She shook her head, incapable of words.

He reached for the object and started to get up from the couch.

Nina gasped when he sank down to one knee.

"I have a question I'd like to ask you, Nina."

She felt welded to the spot, her heart beating a million miles a minute.

"I know you might think it's too soon. But it seems like forever that I've been moving toward this moment." He swallowed thickly. "I love you," he said simply. "And I think you love me, too."

She nodded, although words refused to form in her emotion-filled mind.

"Nina, will you do me the honor of being my wife?"

She squeaked, sinking to the floor on her knees in front of him and throwing herself into his arms.

She kissed him wildly, holding his handsome head steady as she launched an all-out assault on his delicious mouth.

As always, things spiraled quickly out of control, with each of them snatching at each other's clothing, as if unable to get them off fast enough.

Nina knew a moment of clarity as she looked over his shoulder at the front doors.

"Someone might see," she whispered.

"Let them see," he whispered back.

Within moments they were completely nude, still kneeling on the floor in front of the couch.

"So," Kevin said, brushing back her hair from her face. "Does this make it a yes?"

Nina nodded. "Oh, yes. It definitely means yes."

He pulled back slightly, producing the ring from where he'd pushed it halfway up his pinkie finger. She held out her right hand, laughed and then produced her left. It slid on easily.

"I figured we could set the date for six months from the night we first slept together," Kevin said.

She blinked up into his handsome face.

He shrugged. "I figured that's a surefire way to break the cycle."

She laughed and threw her arms around his neck, admiring the ring over his shoulder even as she shimmied her naked body against his, elated by his immediate response.

"Sounds like a plan to me."

Epilogue

Six months later...

NINA SUCKED in her breath and considered her profile in the mirror. Had she really put on weight since her last fitting? Seemed impossible, especially considering the nightly workouts she was getting now that she was living with Kevin.

What seemed even more impossible was that six months had passed since that fateful February night. Was it really August? And were there truly a hundred and fifty guests milling about Kevin's backyard?

"I still think you should have gone with purple."

Nina made a face at her grandmother in the mirror. "White is traditional."

"Who needs traditional?" Gladys's smile as she adjusted the back of Nina's knee-length dress and long veil said she was pleased.

"Stop fussing with that bow already or you'll undo it," Nina's mother said from where she'd come up from behind them, adding her face to the three generations of women in the mirror.

Nina turned to face them both, their ongoing feud serving to distract her temporarily from the butterflies madly trying to escape from her stomach.

"Are you ready?" her mother asked.

Nina glanced out the nearby window. They were already fifteen minutes late getting underway. From here she could see Kevin waiting, glancing at his watch every ten seconds and grimacing up toward the window. He looked both handsome in his tux and absolutely miserable. She smiled, fingering the strand of pearls that he'd given her that morning. Rather, the strand of pearls he'd tried to give her.

Nina was surprised by how sentimental the entire wedding ritual had made her. And she had flown into a panic when she realized she didn't have anything borrowed.

So she'd asked Kevin if she could borrow his mother's pearls. He should keep them to give to their daughter or granddaughter, so could she borrow them for today?

His grin had warmed her to her toes.

And prompted her to tackle him to the bed, uncaring that even that early there were people milling about, from her grandmother and mother to the caterers and the florists.

Sex. If it were true that your interest in it waned with each new partner, she had yet to reach that point with Kevin. And she couldn't imagine ever getting there. Every time was like the first time.

She shivered just thinking about it.

"Uh-oh," her mother said.

"What is it? Did she bust a seam?" Gladys asked.

Nina followed her mother's gaze to find that her taut nipples stood out clearly against the satin fabric of the dress.

"You're not wearing a padded bra?" her mother asked. "For heaven's sake, Nina, have I not taught you anything?"

Gladys smiled at her and Nina gave her grandmother a wink even as Helen rifled through Nina's lingerie drawer looking for a quick fix.

She came back with two thin pads she'd liberated from a demi bra.

"Here. These should do it."

Nina caught her hands. "I don't think anyone's going to be looking at my breasts, Mom. Besides, they won't fit."

Gladys agreed. "You don't want to ruin it, do you? You know, like you have a tendency to ruin everything."

Nina gave an eye roll.

"Fine." Her mother finally relented and sighed. "But for the love of God, please make sure none of the photos come out making you look like that old Farrah Fawcett poster."

Nina laughed. "I'll try, mother."

She moved closer to the window.

"Are you ready now?" Helen asked.

She slowly shook her head and then glanced at the clock.

"Not yet."

She was still waiting for a certain guest to arrive....

KEVIN LOOKED at his watch again. Where was she?

Despite the misters placed around the transformed area, the August temperature had to be hovering at somewhere around ninety. He resisted the urge to drag the back of his hand against his damp forehead even as he stared at the second story of the house. There! There Nina stood in her dress, looking out over the guests.

He released a long breath of relief. At least she hadn't bolted.

But what was happening? Was she suffering from a case of cold feet?

But that couldn't be, because it had only been two hours ago that they had gotten all hot and sweaty—including their feet.

"Kevin."

He froze at the sound of his name. Rather, it wasn't so much the sound of his name, but the sound of someone familiar to him saying it.

He turned to take in the sight of Gauge wearing a suit.

Before he knew that's what he was going to do, he gathered his old friend into a man hug, thrusting his right hand into his to shake it and then pulling him tight.

"Damn good to see you, Gauge," he said. And he *was* glad to see him.

Over the past six months there had been one no-ticeable absence in his and Nina's lives: Gauge.

And now he was here.

He glanced up toward the window to find Nina smiling. He didn't have to wonder who had

found their friend. When Nina wanted something, she didn't stop until she got it. He was
proof positive of that.

"So it worked then," Gauge said quietly,
nodding at the guests gathered.

"What worked?"

"Our plan to get you and Nina together."

Kevin squinted at him.

"Come on, Kev, surely you knew that had
been my intention all along. You two are a
perfect match."

Kevin considered him for a long moment. He
held no hard feelings toward his friend. Too much
water had passed under the bridge to go there.

But he did have a couple of questions of his
own.

"And you and Nina?" he asked.

Gauge stuffed his hands into the pockets of his
slacks. "Beyond friendship, there is no me and
Nina."

Kevin couldn't be sure, but he thought he saw
a shadow of something indecipherable on his
friend's face. Longing? Pain? Had there been a
part of him that had wanted Nina as much as
Kevin had wanted her? Not merely in bed, but
in a relationship?

But then Gauge grinned at him. "Congratulations, man. I know you both will be very happy."

Kevin recognized the genuine emotion behind the words and he smiled back at him just as Edith Christenberry, the church organist and his mother's onetime best friend, struck up "Here Comes the Bride."

Gauge turned to move off to join the guests.

Kevin grasped his arm. "No, please. You'll notice I have no best man. That's because you were the only best man that I would have considered." He tore his gaze away from his beautiful bride for a split second. "Be that for me now?"

Gauge nodded once. "I'd be honored."

SIX MONTHS had changed very little, Gauge realized as he watched his best friends exchange vows. Guilt and sadness and longing filled him as if everything had happened yesterday.

He looked down at his shoes.

What remained was what he was going to do about it.

* * * * *

Wait! The story's not over yet!
Watch for the
INDECENT PROPOSALS *mini-series,*
starting later this year.

Wait!

Kevin and Nina might be settled, but there's still a lot of reckless, sexual energy in the air.

Find out who ends up under its influence next in Reckless *by Tori Carrington, available in November 2009.*

Here's a sneak peek…

1

HOT BREATH CREATED a steamy dampness on her neck, challenging the summer heat for dominance…. Her nipples awakened to tingling life under the sensual attention of his roaming hands…. She tightened her thighs, trapping his hips, a moan building in her throat….

Heidi Joblowski arched her back against the cool sheets and slid her hands down to cup Jesse's bottom, holding him close.

Oh, yes.…

He instantly stiffened against her, his body quaking.

Oh, no.

Not again. Not yet.

Heidi bit her bottom lip, praying that this wasn't it. That Jesse wasn't finished.

He collapsed against her.

The moan turned into a groan.

"Mmm," he hummed, kissing her neck several times and then kissing her mouth. "That was good. You were good."

Apparently she was too good. He'd reached climax before she was even halfway up the ladder, leaving her hanging from the rungs with no hope of his helping her over. Because she knew that no matter what she said, what she did, he was done.

And she wasn't even close.

"What?" he said when she kissed him back with moderate enthusiasm. "Oh, no. Did I do it again?"

Heidi took a deep breath, trying to mentally unwind her coiled muscles. "When I said 'quickie,' I didn't mean it in the literal translation of the word. I meant 'no foreplay necessary.' But an orgasm would have been nice."

He chuckled into her hair. "I'm sorry, Heidi."

She stretched her neck, figuring she could see after herself in the shower. After all, it was three o'clock on a busy Saturday afternoon in June and she certainly hadn't expected more. She had hoped for more, especially since they'd spoken several times lately about Jesse's habit of not waiting for her before diving over the orgasmic edge.

Of course, all it usually took for Jesse was a

gentle blow in his ear and a squeeze of her thighs and he was a goner.

Therein lay the problem.

"It's the place, I think," he said, smoothing her hair back from her face. "It's strange having sex in Professor Tanner's place."

"It's not his place, it's mine. At least for the summer while I'm renting it from him."

Well, she was actually partially house-sitting, as well. Watering Tanner's plants, taking care of his garden and forwarding his mail to him while he was in Belgium for the next couple of months. The perfect trade-off, really. She got the type of privacy with Jesse that she'd never have at home with her parents, or at his apartment, which he shared with two friends, and all she had to do was take care of the house as if it were her own. Perfect.

Only it wasn't working as well as she'd hoped.

Jesse turned on his thousand-megawatt grin. "Do you want to try again?"

Heidi quickly reached for another condom on the nightstand.

A knock at the front door thwarted her intentions.

Jesse kissed her. "I'll make it up to you, Hi. I promise."

She languidly snaked her arms around his neck and tunneled her fingers in his thick, dark hair. "At this rate, you'll owe me well into the next century," she whispered.

His chuckle made her smile. "So be it." He kissed her deeply again before pushing off to jump into his jeans sans underwear. "I can come up with worse debts."

So could she.

Heidi propped herself up on her elbows, watching Jesse Gilbred's fine male form as he got dressed. His tousled hair dipped low over his brow. His slender, whipcord-taut muscles moved and rippled with his actions. His green eyes twinkled at her mischievously.

It was a sight of which she'd never tire. This man she'd met when they'd been little more than kids in high school and had remained with ever since. He'd been the captain of the football team, she'd been the head cheerleader. Even when he'd left Fantasy, Michigan, to attend college in the East, they'd maintained a long-distance relationship, with his returning at least one weekend a month to see her. It had been a long two years, but when he'd graduated and come home for good to work in a managerial capacity at his father's construction company, she'd been there for him, just as she had for the past eight years.

He had been her first. And she intended for him to be her last. He was the one she'd built all of her plans around. Well, all but the little detail they encountered every now and again, as they had just now. But they could definitely work on that.

He left the room, and Heidi pulled a pillow over her head and gave a muffled moan.

"Hey, how's it hanging, man?" she heard Jesse say as he greeted their visitor.

She budged the pillow to peek at the bedroom door he'd left wide-open.

Jesse's best friend entered her line of vision, all blond hair and dark tan. He stared at her, apparently as startled as she was at being caught unawares.

"Jesse!" she called, yanking the sheet up to her chin and then off the bed so she could get up and close the door.

Heidi leaned against the wood for long moments, listening to Jesse's laugh and Kyle's awkward apologies.

So much for seeing to her own needs.

She made out Jesse's words through the wood. "No need to apologize. If a guy can't trust his best friend, who can he trust?"

Heidi gave an eye roll and dropped the sheet, stepping over it on her way to the connecting bath.

NAKED AS THE DAY she was born.

The ridiculous saying came to Kyle Trapper's mind as he raked his hand through his hair, staring at his friend as if he'd lost a baseball or two on the way to the game.

Kyle had yet to move from where he stood in the middle of the small, well-appointed living room. His gaze moved back toward the closed bedroom door of its own volition, as if hoping to catch another forbidden glimpse of Heidi's decadent white flesh. He didn't care which part, whether it was her pert, rose-kissed breasts, her flat, toned stomach or the trimmed triangle of hair that seemed to point toward the V of her thighs like an erotic arrow. Any part would do his starving gaze good.

His friend sat on an armchair, pulling on socks and athletic shoes, oblivious to Kyle's thoughts. And it was a good thing. If their roles had been reversed, he'd have punched his friend.

"Hell, Jesse, do you let everyone see your girlfriend naked?"

Jesse got up and smacked him on the back. "Only my closest friends."

Kyle was not amused.

"What's your problem? You'd think you'd never seen a woman without her clothes before."

"Never that woman."

Never Jesse's girl.

His friend grabbed a T-shirt that was hanging on the back of the chair. "How'd you know I was here, anyway?"

Kyle hadn't known Jesse was there. In fact, he hadn't come here for his friend at all. He'd come to talk to Heidi.

He cleared his throat. "Where else would you be?"

His response must have come out gruffer than he'd intended because Jesse paused. "Hey, you never have told me what your problem is with Heidi, but she's one of the most open women I've ever met." He shrugged as he pulled the cotton over his head. "She won't care that you've seen her naked."

"Right. That's why she slammed the door." Kyle rubbed the back of his neck. "And what do you mean by my having a problem with her?"

Jesse pulled the T-shirt down, revealing the

name of a local tavern. "She thinks you don't like her."

That surprised him. But at the same time, it was cause for relief. If either Jesse or Heidi had a clue about how he really felt…well, suffice it to say he didn't think he'd be standing in her rental house right now, about to leave with her boyfriend to play ball.

In fact, he'd probably be run out of the small town on a rail, back to a life that had never held much for him in the way of a future.

"Anyway, we all know you're gay," Jesse said, lightly hitting him on the arm.

"What?"

"You heard me. I haven't seen you date a single woman since you've come to Fantasy. That, and you weren't without a girl nearly every night of the week back in Boston. I figured you'd switched sides and were batting lefty."

Now that was a new one. But, hey, he figured so long as it kept his best friend from learning the truth, let him think what he would.

"I'm joking, man."

Kyle stared at him, realizing that Jesse had expected something else from him. A denial maybe. Or perhaps a mock physical assault.

He didn't think it was a good idea just then to deny him. He made like he was going to slug him.

Jesse laughed and good-naturedly dodged the hit as he grabbed his ball cap. "Come on. We can get in some practice on the field before anyone else gets there."

Jesse opened the front door and walked out. Kyle stood staring at the closed bedroom door for a long moment, feeling like he owed Heidi an apology or something. He heard the spray of the shower and swallowed thickly, the sound combining with the memory of her sleekly naked body to provide an image he really didn't need. Lord knew it was torture being around her as it was.

The blare of a truck horn sounded from the driveway.

Kyle gave the door one last glance and then reluctantly turned away. If he knew what was good for him, he'd keep on going until he was back in Boston and well away from a temptation that had the potential of destroying all the good he'd finally found in his life.

THE TOWN PUB was a popular gathering place all year round, but in the summer it was doubly so.

Heidi shouted her order to the tender over the cacophony of voices, most of the patrons having come from the baseball complex on the edge of town, like her. She peeled off the money to pay for the beer and then juggled the four bottles as she made her way back to the table. Unsurprisingly, she found that Jesse had left his chair and was playing darts with Kyle. He took his beer from her as she passed.

"Thanks, babe."

He kissed her cheek but his gaze was on the target some ten feet away. She put the remaining beers on the table and sat down next to her friend Nina Leonard-Weber.

Actually, Nina was more than a friend—she was Heidi's boss at the bookstore café she'd been working at for the past year while she finished college. And Nina was partners in more ways than one with the man sitting on the other side of her, Kevin Weber. The two had married a couple of weeks earlier, surprising most everyone with the rapidness of the ceremony. To this day, half the population watched Nina's stomach, convinced she must be pregnant.

Heidi knew they'd married because they were in love.

"When are you going to ask Jesse to stop calling you a pig's name?" Lindsay asked, quirking a brow at her from across the table.

Heidi and Lindsay took the same courses at nearby U of M—well, during the regular term, anyway. Heidi was enrolled in summer courses so she could finish early, while Lindsay had taken the season off to relax a little, she'd said.

Heidi made a face at her as she pushed a beer toward her. "He doesn't mean it that way."

Nina and Lindsay shared a look while Kevin pretended he didn't have a clue what they were talking about.

"Oh, stop it," Heidi said with a laugh.

"Hey, you're the one who pitched a fit when he proposed at the wrong time," Nina reminded her.

Heidi cringed and leaned her forehead against her open palm. "Oh, God, I knew I shouldn't have told you about that."

"If not me, then who?"

Lindsay leaned in closer. "If I wasn't already involved with John, I'd certainly give Jesse's friend Kyle another look or two."

"What are you talking about?" Heidi asked. "You haven't stopped looking at him since we got here."

"I can look." She waggled her fingers. "It's the touching I can't do."

And if John were there, she wouldn't be doing even that without causing an argument. But thankfully John wasn't there.

Lindsay met Heidi's gaze. "Did you really refuse to accept the ring?"

"Of course she did," Nina answered for her. "Ordered him to put it right back into his pocket, she did."

"Whose story is it?" Heidi asked. "Yours or mine?"

"At this point, I wake up sometimes afraid it's mine."

The three of them laughed.

"Heidi has this…idea of how she wants her life to unfold."

"It's a plan."

"Excuse me. Plan." Nina gave her a sidelong glance. "And Jesse's proposing before the appointed time sent everything into a tailspin."

Lindsay sighed. "Most women would be thrilled to be proposed to at all. Much less by a hot guy of Jesse's caliber."

"Yes, well, Heidi's not most women. Anyway, she and Jesse have been a couple for, like, forever. And she'd always seen herself getting engaged…" She looked at her friend. "When?"

"You know when," Heidi said, holding a cold bottle against the side of her face to cool it. "When I get my MBA. What's so wrong with that?"

"Which is when?" Lindsay asked.

"Next month."

"So let me get this straight. When did Jesse propose?"

"Last week."

"So he popped the question a whole five weeks before your idea of when you thought he should propose, and you turned him down?"

Heidi was affronted. "I didn't turn him down. I just told him to ask me in five weeks."

Lindsay leaned in again. "Was the ring big?"

Heidi grinned.

"What do you think? She probably picked it out," Nina said.

Heidi gaped at her friend. "I did not. We just happened to be out window-shopping and…" Her words trailed off and she laughed. "Okay, I picked it out. Tried it on and everything." She looked at Lindsay. "And it's huge. Three-carat marquise-cut bracketed by one-carat yellow diamonds."

"Wow." Lin looked impressed. "And you turned it down?"

"Only for now." Heidi shifted.

Nina counted off on her fingers. "First there's the proposal after she's graduated. Preferably on the night she accepts her diploma. Then there's a one-year-to-the-date marriage with a big wedding at St. Pat's. And nine months after that, their first child."

"You can't plan stuff like that," Lindsay said.

"Why not?" Heidi asked.

Nina shrugged and sipped her beer. "Everything's gone according to plan so far. There's no reason to think it won't now."

"Talking about me again?"

Heidi looked up to smile into Jesse's handsome face, returning his kiss with gusto. "Always."

He pulled up a chair next to her while Kyle did the same on the opposite side of the table. Heidi met his gaze briefly and felt heat suffuse her from the top of her head down to the tip of her toes. She'd avoided looking directly at him since their little…run-in earlier at the house. It wasn't every day someone who wasn't her boyfriend saw her naked.

She wasn't sure what she expected to see. An

apology, maybe? Or perhaps even a knowing smirk?

Instead Kyle wore an expression she couldn't quite define. And for the span of a millisecond she felt the type of electricity she'd experienced only one other time in her life: when she'd met Jesse.

She blinked, shocked to find herself suddenly breathless.

"So what did you guys think of the game?" Jesse asked, flexing his right bicep. "Did we rock or what?"

Everyone shouted responses, both pro and con, as Heidi quickly looked away from Kyle.

She was relieved that when she looked back, Kyle had looped his arm over Lindsay's shoulders.

"Pity the man who has to sing his own praises," he said, smiling down into Lindsay's pretty face.

"And praise the man who doesn't have to," Kevin agreed.

The table erupted into laughter.

Heidi picked up her beer bottle and drained half the contents, feeling oddly like she'd just touched a live wire. And she hadn't a clue as to how she could let it go....

2

KEEP THINGS LIGHT. Keep things safe.

Kyle repeated the words in his mind three days later as he climbed out of his car in the parking lot of BMC, the bookstore/music center/café where Heidi worked. He shaded his eyes, spotting Heidi's old Sunfire convertible parked a couple of rows up. Good, she was working. That meant that he could talk to her in the safe environment of her workplace, safe being a relative term.

At any rate, he was sure there would be little risk of seeing her naked again. It was hard enough seeing her in public, with Jesse, without imagining her without her clothes.

Which made what he was about to ask doubly difficult.

"Oh, for God's sake, she's just a woman. More than that, she's your best friend's girl. Get over it."

But no matter how stridently he censored

himself, he knew that the attraction he felt for Heidi far surpassed coveting his friend's girl. From the moment he'd ridden into Fantasy and met Heidi at Jesse's place, he'd known he was in trouble.

And had done everything in his power to combat the unwanted feelings.

"Kyle?"

He pulled his gaze from Heidi's car to find himself looking at Heidi herself. She was wearing her work apron, the white fabric snugly fitting against her slender frame. It was as if she'd emerged from his thoughts, looking somehow out of place in the parking lot.

He realized he hadn't said anything yet, and managed a simple, "Hey."

She walked in his direction. "What are you doing here?"

He squinted at her.

"Trying to expand your horizons by buying a book?"

He stuffed his hands into his jeans' pockets. "Actually, I heard the clam chowder was pretty good here."

Her smile eclipsed the sun. "The best, considering I'm the one who makes it."

"You going somewhere?"

She looked over her shoulder and then at her watch. "Yeah. I thought I'd get a few errands out of the way during my break."

"I was hoping we could talk."

Now that hadn't come out quite the way he'd wanted. It almost sounded as if what he had to say was personal. While it was, it wasn't something that should have inspired the wary look on her beautiful face.

She looked at her watch again. "I'm sorry, but I really don't have the time. I only have fifteen minutes before I have to be back at work."

Kyle grimaced. Probably he should have just gone in and ordered and waited for her to come back. Now if he did that, she'd likely avoid him at all costs.

Hell.

"It's not what you might be thinking," he said.

"I'm not thinking anything," she said, beginning to walk away. "Why would I be thinking anything?" She shrugged. "You know, aside from it seeming like you've been going out of your way to be rude to me ever since you came to town two months ago."

"Pardon?"

She planted her hands on her hips. "You heard

me. I mean, come on, Kyle, did you think I wouldn't notice that you don't like me very much? I don't know why that is…and I don't want to know. So why don't we just continue on the way we have. You know, with chilly cordiality?"

Chilly cordiality? Now that was a description.

Unending cold showers would be more his choice of wording.

He looked her over. She really didn't have a clue, did she? Despite the other night, when he was afraid he'd revealed more than he'd ever intended to at the bar after the softball game, she thought he didn't like her.

Which usually suited him just fine.

But not now.

"I've really got to go."

She turned to walk away. And without his realizing he was going to do it, he grasped her wrist to prevent her from leaving.

"We really need to talk, Heidi."

HEAT, SURE AND SWIFT, swept over Heidi's skin from the casual contact. A heat she didn't want to acknowledge. There was only one thing worse than the possibility of being attracted to her boyfriend's best friend: knowing that he didn't return the sentiment. In fact, she was convinced that Kyle was not only not interested in her sexually, he wasn't interested in befriending her, either, no matter how hard Jesse tried to push them together.

"I don't know what we could possibly have to talk about," she told him now.

Liar. She could start by telling him how something had changed in her feelings toward him the other night. Something elemental. Something confusing. Something frightening.

Recently Nina had told her that plans oftentimes had a way of not turning out exactly the way you wanted them. That wasn't Heidi's experience. And she didn't want to even consider that her well-laid plans would go any way but right. She'd been raised in an environment where simple things like dinner and regularly paying the electric bill hadn't been planned, so she'd taken it upon herself to impose order on her own life. As soon as she was old enough, she'd gotten herself up and to the bus stop on time, advancing from an often tardy student to one who was always on time. She'd gone shopping with her mother, and while Star Joblowski had lingered in the book section leafing through style magazines, Heidi had consulted a list she'd made of items they needed for the house and meals, not just for the coming week, but two weeks in advance, because she never knew when her mother would think to go to the supermarket next.

She liked order in her life.

And her reaction to Kyle's skin against hers now was nothing if not disordered.

She slipped her wrist out of his grip.

"Look," he said, shoving his hand back into his jeans' pocket, appearing as irritated as she was. "I know you and me...well, we haven't really gotten on well since I moved here. But Jesse would like to change that. And, frankly, so would I."

Heidi frowned. "I'm okay with the way things are."

He looked at her closely. Perhaps a little too closely.

"What is it that you want to talk about, Kyle?" She made a point of looking at her watch again. At this rate, she'd be late returning from break. And she hadn't seen to one of the three errands she'd wanted to run.

"I want you to help me plan a surprise birthday party for Jesse."

"A SURPRISE BIRTHDAY PARTY?" Nina repeated some time later, after Heidi had returned to work.

The two women were in the café's kitchen, Nina sitting on the prep table snacking on oyster crackers while Heidi put all her energy into kneading a fresh batch of sweet dough.

Usually this was one of her favorite times of day, when the morning baking and the lunch rush were over and she could enjoy the afterglow of a job well done and kvetch or gossip with Nina while she tried out a new recipe.

Sometimes it was difficult to remember that Nina Leonard-Weber was her boss. Nina certainly never put on any airs, and always treated her like a coworker rather than an employee. Ideas were exchanged, schedules switched. And there wasn't a thing Heidi didn't think she couldn't tell her.

Her cheeks felt like they were on fire…along with her pants. What was the saying? Liar, liar, pants on fire?

There was one thing she wouldn't dare tell Nina. And that was anything having to do with her recent sexual awareness of Kyle. To do so would not only be the ultimate in recklessness, it would be taking it beyond a real fear to a very real reality.

"So what did you tell him?" Nina popped another cracker into her mouth.

Heidi slowed her kneading. "What was I supposed to tell him?"

"That you had to check your schedule?"

She pinched off a bit of dough and threw it at Nina. "I told him yes, of course."

Kyle had offered a convincing case. Said he wasn't used to doing things of this nature, but wanted to do one thing on his best friend's behalf to make a dent in the debt he owed Jesse for helping him out on so many occasions.

Nina pushed off the counter and threw away the dough stuck to her shirt. "I'd be careful there."

Heidi stopped kneading full stop. "How do you mean?"

"I don't know. You could say that I've had a little experience being…friends with two hot men."

A few months ago there had been rumors that backed up Nina's vague claim, but Heidi didn't much go for workplace gossip, or gossip of any nature for that matter. Wasn't it hard enough to accept truths? Why did anyone want to mess around with half-truths?

Anyway, when the third partner in the store, Patrick Gauge, had left town without warning, a few had said it was because he and Kevin and Nina had become involved in a love triangle of sorts.

The news hadn't impacted Heidi one way or another. The music center had needed a replacement manager, but more than that, she couldn't say why Gauge had left or when, if ever, he might return for more than a visit. And since Nina and Kevin weren't saying anything, she figured it wasn't any of her business.

The telephone extension rang, but Heidi didn't make a move to get it, seeing as she was up to her elbows in dough. She was mildly surprised that Nina didn't even appear to hear it. Someone must have picked it up out front.

"Anyway," Nina said, checking the progress of another bowl of sweet dough that was rising on top of the warm stove. "I just think it's important for you to be careful."

"I'm not following you."

"You know, you might not want to be…alone with Kyle during any of the planning meetings…stuff like that."

Heidi laughed. "Don't be ridiculous. Jesse and I have been a couple for eight years."

"Just the same...."

Janice, the front-counter girl, opened the door a crack. "Heidi, it's for you."

Her throat suddenly went dry. Nina's gaze sharpened on her face.

"I'll finish up," her friend said. "You go talk to whoever it is."

Heidi wiped the dough from her fingers and then quickly washed her hands before picking up the phone in the corner.

"Heidi?"

Her shoulders instantly relaxed and she made a point of saying directly to Nina, who was still watching her. "Hi, Mom."

Then she turned away, not about to admit that she, too, had been half afraid that the call was from Kyle.

She groaned inwardly. How was she ever going to plan a party with the man if she couldn't deal with the thought of talking to him on the phone?

She didn't know. But she knew that for Jesse's sake, she was going to have to find a way....

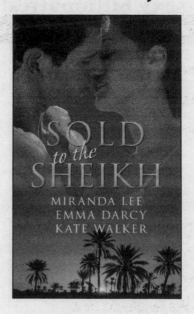

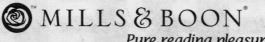

FREE

2 BOOKS AND A SURPRISE GIFT!

We would like to take this opportunity to thank you for reading this Mills & Boon® book by offering you the chance to take TWO more specially selected titles from the Blaze® series absolutely FREE! We're also making this offer to introduce you to the benefits of the Mills & Boon® Book Club™—

★ **FREE home delivery**   ★ **Free gifts and competitions**
★ **free monthly Newsletter**   ★ **Exclusive Book Club offers**
★ **Books available before they're in the shops**

Accepting these FREE books and gift places you under no obligation to buy; you may cancel at any time, even after receiving your free shipment. Simply complete your details below and return the entire page to the address below. You don't even need a stamp!

YES! Please send me 2 free Blaze books and a surprise gift. I understand that unless you hear from me, I will receive 3 superb new titles every month, including a 2-in-1 title priced at £4.99 and two single titles priced at £3.19 each. Postage and packing free. I am under no obligation to purchase any books and may cancel my subscription at any time. The free books and gift will be mine to keep in any case.

K9ZEE

Ms/Mrs/Miss/Mr...Initials ....

BLOCK CAPITALS PLEASE

Surname ....

Address ....

....

....Postcode ....

Send this whole page to:
The Mills & Boon Book Club, FREEPOST CN81, Croydon, CR9 3WZ